The 'Chronic'les Series

Bigfoot06 Publications (OPC) Pvt. Ltd.
B-10,12 Shree Shyam Palace,
Sector 4,5 Chowk, Old Railway Road,
Gurugram, Haryana (122001)
Website: www.bigfootpublications.in
Email: info@bigfootpublications.in

First Edition : July, 2023

ISBN Print Book - **978-81-19512-19-5**

Printed in India

SIGNS

SIGNS

Manik Bandyopadhyay

Translated, introduced, and annotated by
Malini Bhattacharya

LeftWord

First published in August 2021 by
LeftWord Books
2254/2A Shadi Khampur
New Ranjit Nagar
New Delhi 110008
India

Digital print edition, August 2021

LeftWord Books and Vaam Prakashan are imprints of
Naya Rasta Publishers Pvt. Ltd.

First published in Bengali as Chinha, 1946

leftword.com

ISBN
978-81-950310-6-1 (paperback)
978-81-953546-0-3 (e-book)

Contents

Malini Bhattachayra

Introduction

Signs (*Chinha*) is the fifteenth novel written by Manik Bandyopadhyay (1908–1956) and came out first in April 1946 in the New Year (Bengali) number of *Dainik Basumati*, a reputed daily newspaper in Bengali which also brought out special literary numbers. The following January (1947), Basumati Sahitya Mandir, the publications unit of the same concern published it as a book. No second edition of the book was brought out in the author's lifetime; however, a Czech version was published in 1956, together with 16 of his short stories. But as far as we know it has never been translated into English.

There is an entry about this novel early in 1952 in the fragmentary diaries the author used to keep where he talks about an unpleasant encounter with the management of the publishing concern in which he was told that the novel did not have any demand among their readership. Commissioning him and Tarashankar Bandyopadhyay (another equally famous contemporary author) to write experimental novels for the concern had apparently failed as a project. The reference in the diary is to this novel and Tarashankar's *Jhar O Jharapata* (*The Storm and the Fallen Leaves*) as twin narrative enterprises comprising of immediate authorial response to some of the great political events taking place right at the time.

In fact, both these novels, overtly political in scope, refer back to the mass uprising that Calcutta witnessed on and after February 11, 1946, in protest against the sentence of seven years' imprisonment given to Captain Rashid Ali of the Indian National Army. Officers of the INA which Subhas Chandra Bose had led against British rule in India were at this time undergoing trial at the

Red Fort in Delhi. Even earlier, on November 21, 1945, after these patriots had been committed to trial, Calcutta witnessed a similar outburst of popular anger initiated by students, and involving in it large sections of the working people of the metropolis smarting for a long time under repressions of colonial rule. The present novel actually synthesizes the experiences of these occasions which were but indications of major changes in the political scenario.

Between mid-1945 and mid-1946, we witness not only in Bengal, but in many other parts of the country as well, several incidents of direct confrontation between sections of the Indian people, workers, peasants, and students on one hand, and the colonial powers on the other. E.M.S. Namboodiripad, communist leader and intellectual, has described these as signs of a 'mass revolutionary upsurge' from below, an indication that 'the feelings of the Indian people' were against the 'bourgeois class approach of bargain and compromise', even while Congress and Muslim League leaders were striving to win 'Independence for India and Pakistan' through negotiations with the British. According to him, these incidents of mass upsurge were 'considerably influenced by the fighting organizations of workers and other labouring masses as well as the Leftist parties', including the Communists. But the hegemony of Congress was strong. Their self-contradictory efforts to achieve transfer of power through bargaining while seeking to remain in the forefront of mass upsurge, eventually thwarted these spontaneous efforts from below to wage the final battle for Independence. It was further undermined by the terrifying communalist turn national politics was taking at the same time. The streams of mass uprising 'passed through little channels and finally petered out, rather than joining together to make up a mighty turbulent river of revolution'.[1]

Manik Bandyopadhyay had established himself as one of the

[1] E.M.S. Namboodiripad, *A History of Indian Freedom Struggle*, Social Scientist Press, Trivandrum, 1986, p. 885.

most popular and sophisticated practitioners of the realist mode in Bengali fiction from the late 1920s and early 1930s, when his first short stories and novels started coming out. From the early 1940s, however, we find him becoming more and more interested in the political changes of the time, and the manner in which these were manifested in the lived lives, the thinking and the changing practices of the human actors in it. He became closely associated with the Progressive Writers' Association, a leftist cultural organisation from the early 1940s and became a member of the Communist Party of India in 1944. In this context, not only the content of his work but his style as a fiction writer developed in significant ways. In the brief preface to the first edition of *Chinha,* he clearly states that it is a realist experiment in the narrative mode. He refers to its initial publication in the special number of *Basumati* and says that he has made changes and corrections in the book. Then he adds: 'It is written in a new technique. I do not know whether it should be called a novel. I feel that this kind of a narrative, where events happen swiftly within a short time span, requires to be arranged in this way'. [Translation mine]

Presumably, the upsurge of three or four days in Calcutta was over when the author was in the process of writing about it. By the time the work came out as a book, the massive inspiration on the ground was already in the doldrums. Hindu–Muslim violence and the killings of August 16 and after, had transformed the political atmosphere in Calcutta itself and the sense of united resistance and triumph had receded largely to the distance. In the previously-mentioned entry in the diary of early 1952 there are indications that Bandyopadhyay was keen to bring out a second edition of the book, but neither the publishers of the first edition nor a second publisher he approached showed interest. Had the immediacy of great change that this experimental narrative sought to convey palled to some extent? Had harsh reality proved the sense of exhilarating transformations conveyed through it to be liminal? Creative fiction based on the 'here and now' cannot avoid such questioning of the authenticity of its vision. The fact that the author himself was keen to bring out a second edition is proof however that he had no doubts about its continuing relevance.

Contrary to whatever his publishers may have thought about the book after the heady days were over, *Chinha* continued to attract a section of readers, as is evident from the fact that after the author's death, between 1964 and 1991 at least three more editions of the book were brought out by different publishing concerns and the last edition had a second reprint in 1995. But it so happened that the author did not have the opportunity to supervise a second edition in his lifetime. As a result, some of the inadvertences that remained in the first edition could not be corrected and they stayed as they were in subsequent editions, as pointed out here in the annotations. But the question of readership apart, the value of this narrative experiment remains intact over time precisely because it is a realist narrative in the best sense of the term.

It is not a mere account of the incidents of confrontation that took place on Rashid Ali Day. Nor is it a romantic exercise in nostalgia about the revolution that did not happen. The author observes what is known as 'unity of time' insofar as the narrative concentrates on a span of roughly twenty four hours from forenoon of the first day of the upsurge to the afternoon of the second. The chill descending on the streets with the night as described in the novel would fit in either with the approach of winter in November or with its tail-end in February. A number of episodes, sometimes mainly consisting of dialogues or internal monologues, and representing changing relationships among people from different walks of life at various venues in and around the locale of the main action, are woven together on this frame. Such meetings and partings happening simultaneously at different locations are sometimes presented through the use of a kind of narrative 'montage'. Episodic concerns of individuals get drawn into the vortex of the moment of action, and are, for the time being, resolved through it. The narration represents this revolutionary moment witnessed through the eyes of myriads of people who make it, whether by participating in it or by being caught up in it, by remaining on the margin or by trying to use it to their own purpose, or even by resisting it. It is a rare attempt to catch the internal dynamics of the action by focussing on the fast-changing relationships among its speaking, thinking, acting human agents, when the singular motive force of the objective situation is manifested in the multiplicity of responses. The reality of this moment which the narrative captures remains with the reader even as history moves on.

'*Chinha*' in Bengali can refer to either singular 'sign' or plural 'signs'. The translation uses the plural form in the title precisely because of the impression of a multiplicity of perceptions that the narration seeks to convey. It may be noted that there is no direct reference in the novel to Rashid Ali Day which signifies that it is not the incidents of that day in particular which are in focus. As I have said earlier, the context of two separate days, one in November and the other in the following February, appears to coalesce in the narration. Nor is there any specific reference to the INA trials which constituted the immediate issue of protest on both days. Rather significantly, it is the broader sense of the injustice of continuing foreign rule and the overwhelming idea of Independence that are repeatedly underscored; even the children in their dangerous games on the road mouth this idea. The INA's movement represented one of the many strands of national politics of the time which were not supported by national political parties; but the trial of INA officers was an occasion which allowed the yearning for freedom at the grassroots to find united articulation, and brought its pressure to bear on political parties too. The novel seeks to probe into this deeper unifying urge which informs the protest, rather than stay confined to the issue on the surface.

Some impressions of the exciting and bewildering days of November 1945 and February 1946 may be obtained from first-hand reminiscences of participants in it from the Students'

Federation, the students' wing of the Communist Party and from other historical accounts. The Students' Federation played a crucial part on both occasions though the first call of protest on the streets on November 21 had not come from them. They themselves had not expected that such large numbers of students and working people should gather on the streets and go into direct confrontation with armed and mounted police and even the army giving the resistance the look of an insurrection. They did not run away even after rounds of lathi-charge but returned in large numbers and sat on the road patiently for hours waiting for direction from political leaders. Sarat Chandra Bose, one of the most respected leaders of the Congress in Bengal, refused to come and meet the students although various emissaries were sent to dissuade them from confrontation. But even after that, the protesting students leading the gathering refused to disperse. Some military vehicles were set on fire by angry crowds after the firing. But generally, the gathering at the main centre of action behaved patiently and resolutely. Leaders of the Communist Party were on the road themselves, but refrained from taking any decision on their own. Violent repression continued for three days from November 21–23 in which fourteen rounds of firing by the armed police killed 33 people including students and injured more than 200. On the second day, Sarat Chandra Bose came and addressed the students and there was a massive joint rally with Congress, League and Communist flags to Dalhousie Square. On January 2, 1946, the Governor of Bengal sent a message to the Governor-General about the strange character of the unrest; of crowds not to be dispersed even with bullets. They ran away, but soon re-grouped on the scene to start their protest anew.

The protests of February 11, 1946 had much the same character and were only more militant. They started with a meeting convened jointly by Students' Federation and Muslim Chhatra League, sinking their differences; students associated with National Congress also joined the rally as news of lathicharge on students near Dalhousie Square started pouring in. In the words of one of the Communist participants: 'The last hour of the Freedom Struggle had struck—the people had realised it though we had not'. By the evening of February 12, things came to such a pass that the army took over some of the more turbulent localities and people were forbidden to leave their homes. The protesters put up makeshift barricades in many areas and sometimes forced back the keepers of law. Workers struck work spontaneously. People poured out from almost all working-class areas of Central Calcutta to support the students and take on the police. Though unarmed except for brickbats, they vented their anger on military vehicles, setting fire to them. What inspired them was the sight of Congress, Muslim League, and Communist flags waving together over student rallies. Peace squads were taken out by the students and workers to prevent hooliganism. The Calcutta Medical College was flooded with the dead and wounded from police action as the students' union there kept working ceaselessly to rescue and treat the latter. On February 12 and 13 alone, there were 23 dead and hundreds injured as recorded at Medical College Hospital. Women students who had joined the protest also sustained injuries. There are reports of even children being victims of army bullets. Hundreds were arrested from the roads and slums. Enforcers of law and order entered residences to beat up people not involved in protests and to harass men and women.

Manik Bandyopadhyay was an eyewitness to some of this. The spontaneous leadership in the movement coming from below—from the young, the students and the working people of Calcutta, Hindus and Muslims; the overwhelming urge for unity and the example of unity set by the protesters; the brutal character of the repression which suggested the desperation of the British administration; and the sheer indecision of the leaders of national parties—all these aspects of his experience went into his creation. The chronology of the narration retraces some of the actual chronology of events; it moves horizontally sometimes to cover simultaneous happenings; and also goes back and forth all the while tracing the trajectories of individual relationships merging into the moment of unity.

There is also another dimension in the narration which provides it with the thickness of reality even while focussing on the dynamism of the moment. As the narration proceeds, we can almost see parts of the city of Calcutta being mapped out in front of our eyes. Dalhousie Square, the centre of colonial administration, is the main hub of protest action towards which rallies come from many directions. The rest of the map lies stretched between the two main railway stations of the city, Howrah Station and Sealdah Station, with the city of Howrah lying on the other side of the river Hooghly. The new cantilever bridge opened in 1943 has to be crossed to enter Calcutta. Then the story goes winding through the docks, the industrial areas, Calcutta Medical College, the huge mansions of Esplanade and Park Street, to residential areas like Bowbazar and the working-class neighbourhoods of Rajabazar and Park Circus. The fictional map coincides with, and highlights associations with, areas, mostly in Central Calcutta, which feature repeatedly in the memoirs of the days of upsurge.

The context of the World War which had recently ended and of the Bengal Famine of 1943, of course, is woven into the fabric of the novel. The continued rationing of essential commodities and the thriving black market constituting the underside of it are important components of it. More than one reference is there to the 'moral decline' of the Bengali urban middle class which follows from the opportunities opened up for unaccounted income from contracts and commissions. Illegal business in contraband goods and unlicensed premises offering forbidden pleasures thrive in the city; there is at least one reference to a burgeoning flesh trade involving very young girls. As many middle-class people lose their jobs after the War, economic uncertainties are on the rise and this tells upon the student community also. Complaints of indiscipline and rowdyism laid at their door have some truth in them and there is evidence in the author's 1945–46 diaries that he perceived this problem as being related with changes brought in Bengali life by the War. Gangsterism also proliferates in the city under the protective shadow of communal politics sometimes swaying the unorganised poor to lawlessness which gave vent to their anger. It is against this background that the author seeks to work out the changing relationships among people from different walks of life constituting the revolutionary moment.

For a very long time, the hegemonic presence of a substantial Bengali middle class had characterised the city of Calcutta. This class of course always had a crucial role to play in the different phases of the Freedom Movement in Bengal. By all accounts, even in the episode of urban unrest the novel tries to capture, a section of white-collar workers in the city had overcome their class prejudices and fears about getting involved in 'political' matters and had even joined the movement on the streets sharing the anger and sense of grievance manifested in the mass upsurge. There are accounts of the massive rally of students and citizens on 22 November, 1945 through Dalhousie Street being greeted by the clerical staff from the offices of Clive Street and from Writers' Buildings; they came out on the road to join the rally in large numbers. Similar occurrences were also recorded during the protests on Rashid Ali Day.

As a realist author, however, Manik Bandyopadhyay had always been profoundly interested in the complex depths of urban middle-class life and the narrative is unsparing in focussing on the self-contradictions of their class-position, their narrow ethos and self-centred romanticism. At the upper end of the scale of course there are the 'noveaux riches', ruthless entrepreneurs and corrupt government officers hobnobbing with colonisers; these people were either disinterested in or felt endangered by what was happening. Propertied men with ambitious wives aiming at political glory but lacking courage seek to use the turbulence for their own purpose. For petty employees taking bribes and trying to drown their sense of guilt at drinking bars the events offer a possibility of retrieving something of their middle-class idealism, just as the sacrificing mother who seeks jealously to protect her son from politics so that he may build his own career is moved by her own middle-class probity to admit that it may not be possible for him to stay away. At the lowest end of the scale, however, we find those who are going down in life, but still feel they will be able to weather the storm on the strength of their social capital, their pride in their education, their loyalty to traditional values and their resolve to maintain respectability at all costs. The author may be suggesting that the proximity in lifestyle they are acquiring with working people may enable them to overcome the narrowness of their class perception at this moment of turmoil.

The luminous signs of a people's will to unify and struggle towards freedom stand out against the darker weft of the contradictions within the situation. The students who lead it themselves come generally from middle-class background; higher education is indeed an opportunity few can yet afford to avail themselves of. This is what makes the 'good boy' who has been taught from his childhood to pursue his studies and his career single-mindedly wonder what makes his classmates so resolute in their political faith that these things do not matter to them anymore. The young man who has had to take a job leaving his education incomplete seethes because he misses the freedom of a student to stake his life in the movement. In fact, it is the students' capacity to be excited and inspired by an idea that seems to enable them to rise above their class-concerns and to become the most visible interpreters of the invisible swell on the ground. It is this wisdom of the young that comes out in the narration time and again. In the final episode, on the sheer force of their own unity at the ground level, students owing allegiance to the major political parties in the state, compel the leaders to join the rally. Student rallies demonstrating such unity in which the highest leaders in the state of Congress and the Muslim League had to come together at least temporarily featured both in the November and the February protests.

At the same time, the narrative also continually reminds us of the fact that Calcutta is a thriving industrial city and the very foundation of organized resistance lies in strong workers' unions in public and private sectors, which have recent experience of struggles against foreign and indigenous big capital. In particular, in spite of all the havoc being planned ceaselessly all through this period by communal forces, the substantial presence of Muslims, both Bengali-speaking and Urdu-speaking, as a part of the working population still gives Calcutta a genuinely metropolitan character. When Amina, a mother from a Muslim working-class family identifies herself as a 'Bengali' woman and hints at the predicament of all women—Hindu and Muslim, she represents a secular cultural identity which accompanies heightened class consciousness. In the novel, these working men and women are major actors in the revolutionary moment, the unsung heroes and heroines of the hour. The high level of the workers' consciousness, educated by their trade union experience and united militant actions which give a boost to the Freedom Struggle, is not just a matter of fiction but is corroborated by the fact that even during the terrible communal violence of August 1946 in Calcutta, localities where strong workers' unions such as the Calcutta Tram Workers' Union thrived, were saved from bloodbath by their united resistance.

While this movement is represented as being spearheaded by urban youth and urban workers, significantly the narration opens with the death from a police bullet of a boy who comes from a distant village near the Sunderbans and works in a menial capacity at a big emporium in the city. In his dying moments, the waiting crowds on the main road appear to him like the tidal bore on the river near his home just before the moment of bursting ahead. Through this striking metaphorical vision of the dying boy and then through the journey of his parents to Calcutta in search of him, the urban upsurge gets linked with transformations taking place in rural Bengal. We hear of unrest among peasants too which bursts out in sporadic violent action like burning down the police barrack and killing the officer who has abducted a young girl from the village for sexual pleasure. This unrest among the peasantry, surviving the devastations of the 1943 famine which the rural rich used for profiteering, shows changes in agrarian relations which would thereafter grow into the Tebhaga Movement. That is outside the scope of this narrative, but the incidents involving peasants in the village of Madhukhali become an integral part of the narration hinting at the expansive scope of the moment of action.

In one of Bandyopadhyay's last novels, there is an authorial comment which disparages the fashionable idea of 'parallel narratives' juxtaposing scenes from the lives of working people with scenes from the lives of affluent classes to highlight the contrast. He points out ironically that any 'parallelism' is a chimera in a class society. What he emphasizes in his technique of story-telling are integral 'relationships' even between exploiting and exploited classes and this is where his style moves beyond mere delineation of contrasts. The internal dynamics of the social rubric brings people from different levels of society in spite of all the distance between them directly or indirectly in touch with and even in head-on conflict with one another. This happens in the story-telling even when they merely happen to cross one another at some incidental conjunction. These moving relationships constitute the narrative rather than mere events.

For this reason, in his own writings, he refers more than once to his transition as an author from the traditional 'event-centred story' to the 'character-centred story' as he calls it. Such 'characters' in his version are not characters which develop and find their final destiny according to the limited contours of the storyline. They are not traditionally 'rounded off' characters representing discrete individuals. Many details about them do not come in the narrative and remain hazy. Sometimes we are left without a clue as to what happens to them at the end of the story. They are more of dramatic configurations who only breathe and exist and act in sympathy or in antipathy through their moving interactions with one another in the context of the narrative.

When we look at his story-telling technique from this trajectory he describes himself, we understand the true importance in it of the long dialogues and internal monologues, the fact that they are integral to the narration. As one character points out in his own defence in the course of a debate: 'Do not underestimate words'. Words are said to be important because they are our only means for understanding and communicating. In the rapid flux of relationships, it is the use and exchange of words which enables us to understand the direction that these are taking. The schoolboy poet at the sit-in who confides to a recent acquaintance his attempts to put into rhyming words the immediate experience of a brutal charge by the mounted police is in fact only seeking to engage in such communicative action. Some characters on occasions take on something like an authorial role, remaining detached to interpret the complexity of the situation for others. But generally, the author's rare dialogic facility appears in full play in the novel and depends for its success on the living tonalities of verbal exchange rather than on commentary. Whether it be a worker with the experience of previous struggles or a repentant drunkard or a gangster or a corrupt entrepreneur trying to save his own skin or an anxious mother or a young man who is too proud or too modest to admit that he is losing too much blood from his wound, it is through their explicit or implicit inseparability with one another at a particular historical juncture as narrated in the novel that they come alive.

SIGNS

GANESH CAN HARDLY feel the pounding of his own heart.

Overwhelmed by wonder and excitement, it seems he has forgotten even to be frightened out of his wits. In his span of life of twenty-something years, he has neither seen nor could have imagined such happenings, such immense—such terrible happenings involving so many people. It is beyond his conception and his understanding. Yet these happenings between the crowds and the police have absorbed his senses in such a manner that it seems to him as if he feels and comprehends all of it, as if he has himself become the crowd. It is not that he has got stuck in the crowd; from his position at the corner of the closed shop against which he is standing he can easily slip into the narrow lane next to it whenever he wants. But how can he go? He has got transfixed to the spot. His breast heaves, blood runs fast through his veins at the roar of the crowds and the sound of firing. Fear and worry have been cast aside. It is not fear, not even calculations of saving one's own life, but merely the mental habit of having to keep one's distance from troubles that tells him to escape. But even that instinct is blurred. That turbulence can be so static, so steadfast, so unwavering that people do not scatter in all directions while confronting gun-toting forces—is something beyond his comprehension. What kind of trouble is this from which no one tries to run away? So, he thinks of leaving, but his legs remain immobile. If no one is running away, then how can he?

What is more, his heart is filled with keen dissatisfaction and deep curiosity. What kind of miracle is this, the same as if on a sudden the rising tide at full moon in the river Haldi[1] near his

[1] The river Haldi flows along the eastern border of the southern district of Medinipur (now divided into East and West Medinipur) and into the Bay of Bengal close to Sunderbans. The author spent a part of his childhood and early youth here and references to this locale are found in his writings. The district was one of the hubs of the Freedom Movement. In mid-1940s it was suffering the consequences of post-1942 political repression, a severe cyclone, and the Great Famine. In the story, Ganesh's village Madhukhali is near the river Haldi and he has to go to the great city to find work.

home should come to a halt? Nothing could have ever stopped the progress of that man-high wall of rushing water entering with mad roar from the sea which lies at a distance of three kroshas, nothing could have delayed it! Many were the full moon nights when he had quietly lifted the thatch that covered the entrance to his hut and crept out without waking up his parents to wait on the ebb-dried shores of the river for the thrilling appearance of the full tide!

During the day, crocodiles took a sunbath on the mud exposed by the ebbing river. By their look, they seemed the most docile harmless creatures. Sometimes a shark sped like an arrow curving out a long streak through the shallow water to catch its prey. Odd-looking fish of all kinds cavorted up and down in the muddy water. It filled Ganesh with melancholy to look at all these. Oh, this beloved, sad river, which contained crocodiles, sharks, fish, all living creatures, and yet whichever way you looked to the right or the left, the pulse of life was missing. And then, the river came alive, the vigorous tide appeared like the madcap god Shiva himself with his crown of white foam making the universe tremble under his dancing feet. It filled Ganesh too with measureless joy.

Now, if after so many days of having been away from home, that familiar, terrifying, exhilarating full tide with its deep roar came back to his mind on the high roads of the metropolis, why does it seem to halt, why does it come to rest on the asphalt pavements? Why is the rumble without movement? What are these waves and waves of black hair taking the place of that curling white foam?

'Hey, what is the matter? Did you get a bullet? Or is it the baton?'

It is Osman who is asking Ganesh this question. His tone is a little doubtful, but full of concern. The boy is leaning against the corner of the closed shop; it is not clear from where all the blood staining his torn, soiled, homemade slip is oozing out. If it is a bullet, wherever it may have hit him, how can the boy just go on standing with all that blood matting the front of his slip? He has a strange look in his eyes like a dead person come alive and staring dazedly. Looks like a hired porter of some kind, his load resting on the ground next to him.

'What! How should I know, babu?' Ganesh's voice sounds angry 'Babu,[2] are they not going to move?'

Babu! The honorific word grates painfully across Osman's heart. Here he is dressed in a toil-stained half shirt and faded worn blue pants, his feet are bare and he has not shaved for the last seven days. Still he is 'babu' to this boy! That hated word which is an abuse to his ears! Regret for having left his job as tram worker rankles anew in his breast. Osman has felt this continuing regret growing stronger since the success of the last strike action. Not even in the second-class compartment of a tramcar had he ever been abused as a 'babu'!

But of course, this boy is merely a hired porter, probably a migrant from the countryside in search of some job to keep off hunger. That is why anyone apart from porters and beggars is a 'babu' to him.

'Will they keep on dithering, babu? Aren't they going to move?'

Ganesh's voice is now growing indistinct, like the cough-constricted voice of an asthmatic, or the mumble of a tubercular patient choking in blood.

[2] This is one of the key terms in the text having complex nuances. It was originally used to denote the landed gentry upholding feudal culture and living lavishly. In the colonial period however it gradually gets detached from older feudal associations and becomes an appellation for the educated urban middle class, both professionals like teachers and lawyers, and the lower echelons of the colonial bureaucracy. It is definitely a class-term demarcating the middle from the labouring classes and is used by the latter with honorific connotation to address their social superiors; it is also a term used by servants to address their masters. In the text, the term often carries a sense of sharp irony. On the other hand, 'babu' is to be distinguished from 'sahib' which term indicates not just a white man but sometimes an Indian who has adopted a more Europeanized life-style and is therefore one notch above the 'babu'. Once in the text the term 'sahib' is used by Rasul to address Osman, a working man, where it indicates respect for a senior and is free of nuances of class difference.

'But of course, they will move', says Osman with a smile, 'If they have not backed out and dispersed helter-skelter so far, that means this steam-engine is just snorting in impatience to advance, waiting only out of a sense of discipline for the signal for 'all clear' to be given. They will certainly move, only the switch has to be turned on.'

'Even then . . .'. Ganesh tries to raise his thickening voice. At the same time, his knees give way and he slides down grazing his back against the hoarding-covered wall of the shop. His body bends as his head lolls. If the building housing the shop at a corner of its ground floor did not have a high plinth at an angle of which his body had been resting, he would have sunk to the pavement even earlier; that minute during which he could still maintain his half-erect posture would not have been there.

'Are you saying something?'

Osman bends down, taking his face as close to Ganesh's as he can. But all that he hears is the rattle coming from his throat. The people closest to Ganesh are now making a ring around him, pushing back the pressure of the thick crowds to allow him space to fall prone on the road.

Osman uses both hands to tear away the slip clotted with blood. The chest shows no wound, not even a hole. Not a drop of blood has come out of the boy's chest. Then how did the slip come to be dripping with blood?

Hold on, there is also a clot of blood on his left cheek. Blood is oozing through the tousled hair. The wound is hidden by his thick, unkempt locks.

'His life should be saved', thinks Osman.

Maybe he will live if taken to the hospital soon. May be! How should Osman know what sort of a wound it is? Osman does not even know whether taking him to the hospital would save his life; what he knows for sure is that he shall die if there is delay in taking him there.

The effort to save him must be made and he, Osman, would

have to make it. Even as his life's blood was welling out, it was to him that this boy had repeatedly directed his question: 'Babu, are they not going to move?' This is the only answer he had demanded of Osman at his moment of martyrdom. How can he not try to save him?

Ambulance? Some ambulances are waiting just round the corner. He can get some help to carry the lad to that point; he knows that the thick crowd will part, making way for them. But he also knows how ambulances work. For a boy who is a mere porter, the wheels of the ambulance will take so much time to move that he may die before that. No, Osman cannot rely on ambulances.

A ramshackle open truck is standing on the roadside, caught in the rally. Osman stands up and calls, whose truck is it?

Jiwanlal says, 'it is mine'.

'Then in God's name,[3] you are in charge of this boy's life! Take us to the hospital as fast as you can!'

Jiwanlal hesitates only for a moment, then says, 'Bring him along!'

He starts the engine and grasps the steering wheel; in the meantime, Osman has got into the truck helped by willing hands and sits with Ganesh in his lap.

The truck had been caught amidst the crowds, now the crowd parts to make way for it; the truck easily enters the adjacent street and takes speed.

'I HAD NOT wanted to attend the meeting, or to join the rally. Then how did this happen?' Hemanta tries to puzzle out to himself.

His own behaviour seems inexplicable to him, particularly the waywardness of his own thoughts. Once he had walked into the meeting, how could his mind within a short time reject

3 Osman says: 'Khoda kasam', a phrase used by Muslims. Jiwanlal is obviously a Hindu.

without hesitation, without even weighing the pros and cons, the discipline he had observed so strictly for such a long time? All the conclusions he had reached after prolonged consideration seem to have been rendered meaningless in a single day. It is strange that flouting norms he has observed so long with such strong resolve does not worry or disturb him at all.

How can he or any person change his outlook so easily? What makes it seem so natural for him or any person to adapt to new ideas in a trice? Or is it that things that are happening today have nothing to do with personal opinions? Is this a special situation when it becomes a matter of duty to put aside the quotidian rules which apply to ordinary life? Hemanta feels confused by such thoughts.

No, he is not so unenlightened as to think of politics as trivial rubbish. Particularly, in this country politics means the struggle for independence, a struggle spreading across generations. But like everything else, there is a proper time for politics in an individual's life. Even the most worthwhile occupation can be useless if one engages in it before time is ripe. It tends to have unwonted results. The recipe for success is to fulfil as best as one can one's immediate duties.

Even when he had found a place in one corner of the meeting hall, he had been firm in his conviction that it is not for students to attend political meetings. Politics has no place in a student's life. While you are engaged in studies and in building up your career, getting actively involved in politics is as wrong as wasting your time and energy in cards and idle gossip. To a student, it is only as an object of study that politics matters. A student must disengage from turmoil, excitement and clashes of interest and lead the unspoilt and disciplined life of a hermit.

If this is so, then how does he find himself in such meetings? Why does he join rallies and blockade the road determined to continue as long as necessary? It is not that his opinions have changed or that his faith in them has wavered. But he has come to feel more and more strongly that in the present situation, his individual opinion or conviction is of no consequence. This is not the time for such considerations. Under other circumstances, he would serve them with the utmost devotion, but not now. Now he has to do what thousands of students like him are doing together with thousands of ordinary people. There can be neither any doubt nor any difference of opinion in this matter.

Actually, he had been impelled by curiosity when he went to the meeting. He had wanted to see how student groups so much at loggerheads with one another, so busy in their petty internal rivalries, could come together on one platform. Why, has he not seen a large section of young men of his generation going to the dogs? All they understand is indiscipline, rowdy behaviour, smoking cigarettes, teasing girls, cribbing in the examination hall, getting into brawls with invigilators, even on one occasion leading to the death of one of the latter. He knows that this moral decline is the result of engagement with heady politics. This terrible destruction of values among the youth proves his point. Such laxity is bound to grow when people—students or not—neglect their own work to enjoy the intoxication of issues that are of no concern to them. What could be a better excuse than politics for forgetting all discipline and neglecting one's studies to engage in the excitement of rowdyism?

Can you forge unity out of indiscipline? Of what use is such unity?

The morning is bright with the freshness of the winter sun. How fresh do these faces look! How bright are their eyes! It makes Hemanta feel sad. What lamentable misuse of youthful energy and conviction, seemingly perennial nonetheless, undiminished by wastage, unspoilt even by ideals that have gone astray! At one point he had thought of leaving, turning away from their heated oratory. In fact, it would be worse if he had to witness with his own eyes differences surfacing, arguments giving way to blows. Better to learn from the newspapers tomorrow what happened at the meeting.

But it was impossible to leave.

He got transfixed by those lit-up faces, fearless eyes, the bits and pieces of conversation that came to his ears, the chorus of voices raised in slogans and a strange turmoil of feelings.

Among the speakers there are three boys known to Hemanta. Hemanta feels an upsurge within his breast not only after listening to what they are saying but out of wonder and excitement at the new knowledge it gives him about boys with whom he is already familiar. Their presence and their participation itself had hardly seemed credible to him even after he saw them with his own eyes and listened with his own ears. Take Suddhosatto for instance, who had caused him much heartburn by beating him to the first position in the last tests in his honours subject. Even Sibnath and Anwar—their success in examinations can evoke envy among the circles of the most meritorious students. How do they fare so well in their studies and maintain a regular disciplined life even while taking part in politics and in all the cultural activities of the students?

His mother's face as well as Seeta's comes to his mind. He can hardly get a clear picture of the former in his imagination as he sits on the pavement; she seems to be staring with her large terror-struck eyes at him actually facing the batons and the rifles of the police. Apart from her eyes the rest of the face gets blurred in his mind .The promise he had made to his mother has been broken at last today and broken irredeemably. The ultimate disaster his mother could think of was that he would neglect his studies if he got inducted into politics—his career would suffer, perhaps he would be put in jail for six months or even a year, this had been the extent of her worry. But she has never imagined in her wildest dreams that he would be facing death as he is doing today. Surely her blood would turn cold if she were to know that her son who has to this date followed to the letter her bidding not to go to political meetings has suddenly gone so far out of his mind that not satisfied with joining the rally after the meeting, he is now in the middle of the violent melee waiting to be shot down.

Why, his mother is overcome by nervousness even to think that he may have developed the habit of smoking![4]

Only yesterday Pankaj had plied him with a cigarette, saying, 'Here, good boy, brighten your intelligence with some smoke!' The nickname 'good boy' had been invented for him by Seeta and heartily endorsed by his friends. Hemanta does not smoke; he does not even have the bad habit of chewing betel-leaf. He had put the cigarette in his pocket. Today when after lunch he had put on his shirt just before going out, he was reminded of it and possessed by some whim had found a matchbox, lit the cigarette and taken a comfortable puff sitting on his wooden chair. But in his effort to imitate Pankaj he had started coughing and had thrown it away in a corner of the room where it lay smouldering. As his head was swimming a bit, he had sat down on the chair again to recover.

His mother had gone pale on entering the room, she had smelt the tobacco. She could see that there was nobody else there; yet Hemanta could feel her worried eyes going around the room; she would have felt reassured if there had been someone else with him.

'Why, haven't you gone out yet?'

He could understand how much effort it cost her to hide the tremor in her voice.

'I am just leaving. Give me a glass of water'.

Even after he had put the glass down, she could not bring herself to ask him about the cigarette and reined in her irrepressible urge fearing what answer she might get. Suppose he admitted

[4] To Anurupa's middle-class parsimonious ethics, smoking, chewing betel leaf, playing cards, dabbling in politics, are all vices leading to the wastage of money and energy by students who should make the best of the rare opportunity of getting higher education and concentrate on building their careers. These vices in her view are associated with the 'moral decline' among students that her son also speaks of. Anurupa has been bringing up her children on her own by giving music tuitions. Another character, Ajoy, has to give up college and take a job. These are examples of hard-up sections of the middle class making sacrifices to ensure higher education for their sons (not so much their daughters). No wonder, Anurupa's over-protective dreams about her son take a jolt when she suspects he has started smoking.

that he had taken to smoking. Suppose he got angry with her interference, because after all which young man of his age did not smoke a cigarette or two? Her timid looks turned repeatedly to the smouldering cigarette lying in the corner of the room and she kept on raising her eyes to her son and then lowering them.

Then they brimmed with tears. Hemanta exclaimed anxiously, 'Now you have started crying, Ma! Do not worry, I do not smoke. Pankaj gave me a cigarette and just in a moment of whim I took a pull or two. It did not suit me, so I have thrown it away and that is all!'

'Oh', said Ma with relief, her smile returning to her face, 'Do you know why I cried? Not because you were smoking, but because I thought that you were hiding it from me knowing it to be wrong, that you had dropped the cigarette in a hurry when I entered the room! Otherwise if you think it is alright to smoke, Hema, if you smoke because you want to . . .'.

Then she wiped her smile together with her tears from her face with the end of her sari.

'So now you have nothing to worry about?'

'Only that this is how habits are formed, Hema, even against your wish'.

HEMANTA FEELS A deep sympathy for his mother, and yet at this moment, a peculiar sense of detachment overwhelms the concern and anxiety that goes with that sympathy. Ma seems to be far, far off. If he takes a tramcar from this place he can get home in just fifteen minutes, his mother is perhaps waiting for him with bated breath, yet a gigantic reality seems to stand inexorably between this hard pavement on which he is sitting and that familiar nest around which hovers his mother's deep affection, unlimited good wishes, endless anxiety, as in worlds divided between war and peace there is a sense of close proximity and at the same time of immense distances and contrasts.

Is it not possible to get back home now? After all, for the first day has he not already done enough? But he shakes his head to himself.

No, he cannot leave this place on his own for his individual need. If he had not come, that would have been different. But now there was no going back. For his mother's sake he should return home without delay; if backing out on that ground was just a matter of having a black mark on his personal self-esteem he might have endured even that. But what right did he have to inflict defeat on these others? Suppose he gets up and leaves, what if even one or two others do the same following his example?

SEETA'S THOUGHT ALSO crosses Hemanta's mind. She too seems to be as far off as his mother, as much hidden in mist. Seeta's eyes are not large like his mother's. Perhaps that is why they seem to lie beyond the borders of his imagination. The sharp irony of her low tones, her sudden bouts of gravity, her words full of bitter melancholy and pungent sympathy, her occasional faltering look as if she cannot quite make out what sort of a creature Hemanta is—all these seem to belong to the distant past and he can only hang on to memories of his own reactions to these.

Yet he had met Seeta earlier today.

'Hello, good boy', had been her welcoming words, 'Feeling sorry because there are no lectures today? What is to be done? Not everybody can be happy just amassing knowledge—some also wish to protest against injustice!'

Seeta's words today had a sharper edge than mere mocking banter. It seemed as if she had even become doubtful of Hemanta's humanity. She had never agreed with his opinions and been somewhat contemptuous of his cold conservatism, but so far she had also respected his steady determination, his easy tolerance and his love for his long-suffering mother. Today, Hemanta felt, that respect too was on trial, Seeta seeming incapable even of tolerating him.

'But of course we have to protest against injustice!'

'What then?'

'Neglecting studies is wrong, tolerating injustice is also wrong!'

'What then?'

That revealed the secret of Seeta's anger. 'Will you go on using your opportunistic ideals as a cover for selfishness? Are you refusing to admit that even a student has to be vocal today in supporting this country-wide protest against injustice, even at the risk of being dubbed political?' this is Seeta's question to him, even if she has not put it in words.

This unuttered question must be answered. Sadness fills Hemanta's mind. Will Seeta understand what he is trying to tell her?

'You put me in a fix, Seeta', Hemanta begins, 'You cannot take seriously even my serious words'.

'Oh words! All you can think of is words!'

'But what else can you do? Even protests must come through words'.

Did Hemanta know at that time how easily and how inevitably words which come from the deepest recesses of the heart culminate into practice, how vocal protest turns into life-endangering action?

When Seeta remained silent, he said once more, 'Do not underestimate words, Seeta! If human beings were wordless, the world would have been different. I shall not go into high philosophical discourse; I am only asking you to give me a patient hearing. You know, I do what I say. I am not one for verbal tricks, nor do I speak empty words.'

'Oh I am listening!'

'But will you understand what I say?'

'You can try'.

A hostile silence descended between them for a while.

Then Hemanta took courage and said, 'Indeed, we have to protest against injustice, but protest too has to take note of the circumstances. Suppose when we are together, someone comes and insults you; my protest then of course shall be with my fists.'

The reference was to an incident in the past. Hemanta was not sure why he had to hark back to that story of his own heroics to explain his point today. Perhaps it helped to make his point clear, but he could have gone about it differently.

'Indeed, good boy, I have not forgotten and am grateful for it!'

Her words were like whiplash and Hemanta had to take it. 'Not so, but try to understand why I drew that example. I protested that way on that occasion because it was my duty to protest. But in our state of political subjection thousands of cases of injustice take place every day, if I have to protest each time then where do I stand? There are 400 million people in this country and you know very well what a small percentage of them have the opportunity as we have of getting education. In this situation is not educating ourselves the most effective form of protest for us? Is it not itself a struggle? This country sorely needs educated people, should those of us who got that opportunity spoil it by getting involved in all this strife?'

Seeta looks at him with keen animosity.

'Do you even realise, good boy, that those who go through education like that, keeping themselves immune from everything, do not do so thinking of their country's need, but because their real goal is to pass out, build their career and lead a comfortable life themselves? Your logic is not different from the logic of swadeshi capitalists who excuse their own sins with the argument that this is the only way to take the country ahead on the path of development. Those who are in the student movement understand the importance of education more than you do. It is they who tell the students that they must put discipline first, that they must put their best foot forward to take whatever opportunity there is of getting educated, that examinations must not be neglected. But does that mean they shall have no role in the struggle for independence? That they should have no right to voice their political opinions and that they should not get together to advance their demands—to strengthen their discontent and their love for their country?'

'Oh but is not the result of that too evident in the student community?'

'What result? That they are fighting among themselves and getting corrupted? Are such things the result of loving the country, of wanting independence and carrying on efforts to bring the student community together? You are only giving abstract arguments without understanding the matter in its depth. You have only an eye for defects, but you do not even wish to know what causes them. You think whatever you say is right and it gives you satisfaction to set up imaginary reasons and imaginary targets to attack.'

'That is not my fault, Seeta, if I am only looking at negative aspects it is because positive signs are negligible!'

'Fine, Hemanta, why don't you go now?'

Hemanta was dazed with searing anger; but only for a short while. It was difficult for him to accept that Seeta had merely tolerated him for such a long time and that now at last her patience had come to an end. Seeta would never have him accept without demur whatever she said. Their differences of opinion go back a long time. Many times their exchanges have generated much greater heat compared to which today's confrontation seems mild enough. But then, how could Seeta find him so intolerable today? Had she come to some decision about him after which it is no more possible for her to have patience with him? Hemanta had already tried to work it out in his own mind, but with little success. At last, he had decided that he was only complicating matters. Perhaps for some reason Seeta was not in a good mood today. Was it not natural that people should have such fluctuations of mood?

But now the mystery of Seeta's sharp aversion has become a little clearer to him. He feels it unravelling. No doubt his reactions have been too conservative. The world had really changed a great deal. Today right in front of his eyes he has seen things happen which he had not even imagined earlier. The changing situation has changed the people of this country in many ways, even the students. There are new thoughts, new ideals and a new inspiration which cannot be ignored any more. He alone has so far remained untouched. Because his own mind had lagged behind he had fancied with eyes and ears closed that the country was still stuck in the rut where his out-of-date convictions would have it remain.

This unthinking conservatism had hurt Seeta. She could tolerate difference of opinion with open-mindedness, but this die-hard attitude was too much for her.

THE MOUNTED POLICEMEN are returning after beating back the crowd. The boy next to him says: 'How beautiful these horses are! Look at the rhythm of their hooves beating together and their muscles dancing like waves!'

He must be in his mid-teens. He is very slim, very fair and quite tall for his age. He has wrapped himself up in a shawl very comfortably as if he has come to enjoy a musical or a theatrical performance or some film show.

'Do you know how lavishly they have to be groomed?' Responds the spectacled young man solemnly. His eager eyes are moving in all directions as if he is weighing, calculating and judging the implications of the small and big events and situations emerging around him.

'I would have so loved to pat one of them on the back', says the tall boy half to himself, 'Who knows, they might have broken my head if I had tried!'

Would they? Narayan has some doubt in his mind about that. All that this green boy has seen are the sturdy muscles dancing under the smooth pelt of the horse skirting around them, but it has not escaped Narayan's eyes that the Indian rider astride it for all his huge headgear, large moustache and masterly carriage had betrayed some reluctance, some hesitation, some hidden caution in the manner in which he was guiding the horse. Narayan has seen these people many times on the football ground dispersing unruly crowds in quite a brutal fashion. Their manner of functioning today seems to be different.

But did he really see this or is it merely his imagination? Or perhaps, this is their usual method for dispersing an agitated crowd on the main road.

Whatever that may be, a good number have been injured in the operation.

'Oh—Look at that'!

The tall lad has risen on his knees and is stretching his neck to stare with wide eyes following which Narayan also sees an injured youth further down on the road writhing in agony.

Narayan's eyes burn in anger and the words come out of his mouth like flames, 'It was that officer wearing the hat, why don't they drag him down and tear him to bits? Why are we sitting so quietly? He must be dragged down . . .'

Narayan's voice chokes.

'Now—what a thing to say!' The boy slowly turns his head towards him and looks at him with his large eyes, such beautiful eyes they are!

'But don't you feel the same, Khoka?'[5]

'My name is Rajat'.

'Rajat? Your name is Rajat? Don't you want to drag that man down too and to tear him apart?'

'Oh, I do and so do the others. But what is the use of wanting? Can you do anything you want to do?'

Narayan is a bit taken aback to hear this slip of a boy talking like a ripe old man. He knows whatever argument he may put forward

[5] Khoka is an appellation for a boy-child and a favourite nickname for male children. Rajat bridles at being called 'Khoka' precisely because he is only too aware of his extreme youth and suspects that he is being patronised as a mere schoolboy.

this boy will assume the manners of an old man in answering. Still he says, 'Would they dare to do such things if all of us rushed at them together and trampled them down?'

'Oh, they would love it. Don't you see?' Rajat speaks with sadness; his regretful, pedagogic tone gives Narayan a strange feeling. 'They would be really happy if we turn violent; that is what they want. We are not just us anymore; we are this country. They know there will be an eruption if they hit too hard. So they are suppressing their anger and provoking us—so that we lose our heads. They can flatten us in two minutes if they want to. Then why are they not doing it? As soon as we turn violent we shall just be ourselves and not all the people of our country. Then they will say we died because we broke law and order.' Rajat purses his lips and makes a sound of exasperation. 'This is the problem with hot-headed people like you. You always tend to jump up and down without understanding the situation.'

Narayan feels a churning in his head. This boy has just graduated from boyhood and is stepping into youth, and yet it seems he has attained all the wisdom that is contained in the Vedas and the Upanishads of our own time like the boy-sages of yore of whom we read in the Puranas. If a mere boy can say such things, then why should the story of Parasara, posthumous son of Shakti, bringing back his grandfather Vashistha from the path of self-destruction by uttering the Vedas from his mother's womb seem so incredible?[6]

'Which class in your school do you belong to, Rajat?'

[6] The legendary Parashara is the son of Shakti and grandson of the great sage Vashistha. Before Parashara's birth, Shakti is killed by a king-turned-demon through a curse; Vashistha, about to commit suicide in his sorrow, is stopped in this desperate act when Parashara starts reciting Vedic hymns from the womb of his mother, Adrishyanti. It is the precocity of the still unborn Parashara that is recalled by Rajat's words of caution to someone who is older than him. There are also some associations here with boy-sages such as Uddalaka-Aruni and Nachiketa in the Upanishads, who were endowed from an early age with a high degree of wisdom and passion for truth.

'Does it matter?'

'Don't be offended', says Narayan pleadingly, 'It really doesn't matter, my reason for asking is something else'.

'And what is that?'

'It is that such things are not taught in schools and yet you understand them so wonderfully well, from where did you learn all this?'

Pat comes Rajat's reply: 'Oh I learnt them on my own! Some of it comes from my didi, my elder sister'. Then bringing his mouth close as if disclosing a big secret, he says in a low voice, 'That is my didi sitting there. Please don't look because she does not know I am here'.

Narayan says solemnly, 'But, Rajat, I think she has seen you'.

He had thought that Rajat would be a bit shaken to hear that, but he only makes the same sound of exasperation from his pursed lips.

'Oh, has she? How did you know?'

'Didn't you hear? She called you by your name two or three times'.

Rajat's nature, it seems, is not to hesitate even for an instant on any matter.

He cranes his neck towards the place where his sister is sitting and shouts, 'What is it, didi, were you calling me?'

'Come this side, I have something to tell you', says Shanti.

'How can I?' protests Rajat, 'I have to keep my place here'. Then in a louder voice, 'We can talk when we get home, alright?'

After many days, Narayan feels a kind of relief, as if the intense pain of despair has left him. He feels strong and able. The intolerable pressure of anger which seemed about to crush his whole being, he feels, is getting metamorphosed into power of action. The precipitating hatred, vivid and heart-rending, which keeps him restless all the while and maddens him whenever stirred anew, is now like powerful vapour building up inside the iron boiler of his being, the wheel is about to move now. Are not all the people here, including that slip of a boy, inspired by the same hatred? But that hatred is no more the hatred of the vanquished, scorching itself to death in fruitless self-torment, it is the source of inspiration for victory.

Rajat has been still staring with a questioning look at the spot where the injured youth had been twisting and turning a little while ago; he has now been removed, but Rajat is looking more pensive now than he had seemed to be since his talk with Narayan.

'Are you going to get a scolding from your sister when you get home?'

'Why? Why should she scold me?'

'Then why are you so thoughtful?'

'Oh that!' says Rajat in rather shy and mild tones, 'I was thinking if one wanted to write a poem on him how would one write it?'

'Poem on whom?'

'That injured boy who was twisting and turning there!'

'Do you write poems?'

'I do, but I do not publish them. Didi says you should not publish until you have matured with practice. Now look, suppose I start with this: The great horse dancing with his white rider moves/ and youth lay bare their breasts beneath the hooves—no, this will not do at all. Why should they lay bare their breasts? It is not a matter of idle fancy for them! Still . . .'

Rajat continues to think.

RASUL LOOKS AT the goings-on and thinks, they are preparing for lathi-charge.

The long-healed wound on his right brow itches. That mark will not vanish nor will its memory so long as he lives. May be the memory will fade before death comes, but until he himself turns to earth inside his grave the mark shall stay.

'Abdul, it seems they are about to start lathi-charge!'

'Indeed! Then give me a cigarette, let me have a smoke first!'

The permanent mark on Rasul's brow also came from the blow of a lathi. It runs from the right side of his forehead hidden in hair to just above his right eyebrow. Rasul still finds it hard to believe that saving people from death can bring such reward. During the Great Famine he had left his college course incomplete and had gone back to his own village to see if he could save at least a few people. Chirabagi was the name of his village. Chapalakanta Basu was the landlord. Three days after he had reached there he had had to perform the last rites of his mother who had not died of starvation but of disease.[7] But he had not been disheartened by this sudden mishap; he had made all arrangements to open a relief-centre there. Then one day Jiauddin, a minor local retainer of the landlord came to meet him. Eighty per cent of the residents of the village were Muslims. The official manager of the estate was Nakur Bhattacharji, but Jiauddin ruled the village so that the worst forms of oppression could be resorted to without incurring the allegation that Hindus were oppressing Muslims.

'What is all this about opening a relief centre in this village? Go and do it elsewhere. The landlord does not want any such trouble-making here!'

People were dying in hordes of starvation; to try to keep some of them alive was being called 'trouble-making'! The rub lay elsewhere. If there was a relief-centre in the village, if there were organised efforts to save people, Chirabagi would be likely to come under the scanner. Income from his landed property having been depleted, Chapalakanta had gone into business. Who knows but that relief activities in the village would expose the murky secrets

[7] There is an inadvertent change in Rasul's personality later in the narrative. The author seems to have forgotten midway through the story about Rasul's village links and the reference here to his dead mother. The injured Rasul walks home from the hospital to visit his mother Amina. We also hear of his father, apparently an urban worker himself who has been in jail for the last few months. Generally however it was not unusual for working class families to have their roots in the village, as in Osman's case.

of hoarding, black-marketing and other underhand dealings in which he was involved? Who knows but that there might be one or two government officials who were not amenable to bribe?

But Rasul was not to be stopped. He had set up a shack for the relief centre, had collected food grains and had built up a team of volunteers without coming to the forefront himself. The day before the relief-kitchen was to start he had made preparations for a meeting on the grounds next to Laldighi again keeping himself in the background. Neither did he know how at that meeting called to provide relief to the famine-starved a riot had started nor how police forces in their red turbans appeared out of the blue once trouble had broken out in a corner of the grounds. Just before a lathi cracked his skull and he fell to the ground seeing stars in front of his eyes, the momentary impression of the face below the red turban, distorted with inhuman vengefulness, got stamped into his mind.

Why such vengefulness? What did this terrifying violence mean? It did not fit in even with the pattern of injustice and unreason with which the world is familiar. It seemed to surpass even that. So they had been ordered to crack one or two skulls, they might just have done that. Sense of power might have brought intoxicating pleasure to the act, his disobedience might have pumped anger into the veins of the keeper of law; all of this he could have accepted as appropriate to the situation. But what kind of a blind unnatural mania for revenge was this that it seemed that it was the persecuted person himself who had been the perpetrator of torture over the ages, that he had maddened his adversary by continuously subjecting him to intolerable agony?

Rasul still does not know the answer to the riddle. But it has been indelibly stamped on the page of his mind in burning letters of exasperation.

At first the angry roar of the assembled crowd had created a deafening medley. Now it has been toned down to some extent to constant murmur. The crowds have felt the influence of the disciplined movements of the students and their calm and controlled behaviour. The chance that they might erupt into chaos is no more there. Rasul is surprised by the lack of fervid excitement; but he feels deeply energised. These people are brimming with anger and rebellion in their hearts, but their heads are cool. Rasul feels as if for ages he has been praying for this combination of impassioned hearts and cool heads for the people of his country and today he can see his wishes turning into reality.

The sergeants are standing in a row in their well-tailored expensive uniforms. What are the thoughts that lurk underneath that regal air of assurance and the uncaring arrogance that is expressed in their body language? Poor fellows, all they have are the pride and glory of this job that has been created specifically for them, which enables them even as they tread the soil of the land of their birth to bask in their affinity with that seven thousand odd miles distant island. They remind Rasul of the two swans domesticated by Nurul of Chirabagi.[8]

As for the native forces, they are standing like inanimate puppets. They are yet to receive the order to charge. From one of the side roads a car is seen to advance edging through the crowds as far as possible and as it stops a most embarrassed-looking gentleman in a highly flurried and excited state gets down and looking quite helpless pushes through the people towards the area cordoned by the police. Even on this winter day he is wearing a fine linen kurta although he carries a cream-coloured expensive shawl on his shoulder. Perhaps it was in anticipation of this arrival that the order to charge had been kept pending.

He waves his hand and explains something to the leader of the sergeants, then with great difficulty climbs into a police vehicle.

[8] The reference here is to the Eurasian sergeants who were born in India, but still feel that they belong not to the country of their birth but to the distant colonising country. They are like the swans which, despite being domesticated, are alien to Chirabagi. They are compared to swans also because of the sleekness of their dress and deportment.

Must be some leader whom Rasul cannot recognise.

'Who is it, Abdul?'

'Looks familiar, but cannot quite place him . . .'.

The gentleman stands on the truck for a few moments getting back his breath and then shouts at the top of his voice: 'This is an order from Basanta Roy[9] himself, people should go back home and refrain from making trouble!'

Thousands of voices roar back: 'Let Basanta Roy come himself! Who wants advice? Where is the trouble? We are sitting quietly and shall go on sitting as long as necessary. We do not need advice!'

The gentleman again descends from the truck with a great deal of effort, speaks to the leader of the sergeants with his hand waving and pushes through the crowds in the same flurried manner towards his car waiting on the side road.

Calm descends on all sides once more.

Abdul says, 'Now I recognise him, it is Amritbabu, one of Basanta Roy's hangers-on. You find him in all the meetings, fancies making speeches, but neither gets the chance nor is a good speaker'.

'Then why send such a man?' Rasul asks in an irritated voice.

'He was the only one available, perhaps!'

'But it was unwise to send someone just like that with an order to disperse—he should have come and seen for himself . . .'.

'As if he cares', Abdul contemptuously responds.

There is no ruckus, no turmoil, yet the closeness of the atmosphere is getting oppressive, as Rasul senses it. The test of patience has reached a climax.

[9] The reference is to Sarat Chandra Bose, one of the most respected leaders of Congress in Bengal at the time. By all accounts, on November 21, 1945, when there was a united outburst of student anger on the streets of Calcutta in protest against the incarceration and trial of the leaders of the Indian National Army and there were deaths from police firing, Bose refused to come to the place of occurrence to guide the students. Evidently, he did not wish to get involved in the spontaneous upsurge of anti-colonial anger. When he turned up at the rally the next day, his speech asking students to withdraw their movement failed to pacify their raging sense of injustice.

Abdul says, 'Perhaps the lathi-charge will not take place after all!'

'Who knows?'

'Where will it culminate? Are both sides going to sit quiet?'

'Is that possible? One or the other side will lose patience and break out.'

'But we are sitting quietly. They cannot start charging without provocation either, then?'

'Let us see, are you afraid?'

'No why should I be? I am not alone.'

That statement fills Rasul with happiness. It is not strikingly new, but because it tallies with his very thoughts and seems to echo them, it sounds particularly sweet. Rasul does not know who that great hero is who feels no fear when faced with pain, losing blood, may be death? Yes, he feels fear quite strongly; he has to force himself to keep it in check. All he knows for sure is that fear has never been able to overwhelm him, but he would feel ashamed to boast that he has never felt fear. He is quite happy that he does not feel the urge to claim greater heroism than this either for himself or for the others. But today fear and worry seem to have been dissipated. A new self-confidence was surging in with a feeling of unstinted courage. Abdul's words have proved that they are feeling alike; he is not alone. Whatever lies waiting for him—the pain of injury or the closure of death—it shall be shared with many others.

The lathi-charge starts a little later.

It is not something unfamiliar to Rasul. Chaos, shouting, people running helter-skelter—but in the midst of all that he realizes that apart from hurting some unarmed young men and boys this lathi-charge is not going to serve its purpose. Those who have decided to stick it out would not back down as a result of it. Two policemen advance towards him; of course they have no time to pick and choose, nor is there anything to pick and choose in this crowd. Rasul stares at the man unblinkingly; all of them are familiar to him, their faces formed in the same mould.

He raises both arms to protect his head. The stick falls close to where his arm is joined to his shoulder, but only the lower end of it. The hand that is gripping the stick deliberately hits him not with the tip or the middle but the lower end. He feels pain of course, but Rasul is oblivious of it. His eyes are fixed on the face below the red turban. At the fall of the stroke he clearly glimpses that face winking at him before passing on.

'Abdul! Did you see?'

'What? Did that hurt? I hope you have not broken something?'

'Oh, no! It did not hurt in the least! But didn't you see?'

It happened in an instant; he does not know if he saw right. Perhaps it was an accident that he had been hit by the lower end of the stick. Yet crouching on the wide road Rasul keeps on chanting to himself that he has won freedom at last, his course is now unhampered wherever in this land of his birth he may go—in the sky, on the ground, in the depths of mines or on high seas. The breeze is sweet to his nostrils. The touch of the asphalt under his feet is different. The natural flow of his mind had been arrested ever since that meeting in his village, that day had imprisoned him within the bounds of a life static and wretched—surrounded by the curse of oppression, morbidity, corruption and despair. But all that has changed now. Even the dull darkness of his heart is throbbing with a new consciousness. The tide is filling up its stagnant pools.

Has the old mark on his brow disappeared? It is not itching any more. The doubt which had plagued him seems vague and inconsequential. Why had he felt so troubled for so many years by the out of the way maniac behaviour of a single person? Such things happen, they are not out of the ordinary. Only a person who has isolated himself from the rest of the world can destroy himself without doing anything wrong, or behave like a demented animal out of self-hatred. Even a murderer who has knifed his victim remains just a murderer until he has forsaken the company even of other murderers. Only then does he turn into a pervert, a total monster.

'Abdul, something is about to happen!'

'But what?'

'Oh, something big, can't you see them getting restless?'

At that moment the sound of firing starts and Rasul's right arm suddenly seems to jump up violently on its own and then drops useless to his side.

Abdul says, 'Let me see where it hit you!'

'Where else? My bad luck, it is my right arm.'

Both of them are wearing loose pyjamas. A boy quickly comes up, tears an end of his own dhoti and after stuffing his handkerchief into the wound, starts tying up the arm tightly with the torn piece of cloth.

Rasul goes on speaking, 'Now I shall have to practice doing everything with my left hand; never mind, I can ride my bicycle to the college using just one arm!'

TODAY IS THE last day, thinks Akshay, he will just have a drop and end it.[10] He would not touch the stuff again for the rest of

[10] It is tempting to surmise that Akshay's struggles against his demon, drunkenness, bear reference to the author's own alcoholism in his later years. But while there may be some personal reasons for the author's interest in a character like Akshay, the crucial differences between the fictional and the personal must not be overlooked. Akshay is not quite an alcoholic. His dependence is largely emotional, fuelled by his self-degrading sense of guilt. It is not a physiological dependence. In the case of the author, the context of his becoming dependent on alcohol may be found in his being subject to epileptic fits from 1935, a period of over-intense creativity for him. The tranquilising drugs which he had to take to avert such fits, he felt, impaired his creative urge and he started taking alcohol regularly immediately after tranquilisers to keep himself from being reduced to a 'vegetative' state. This deadly experiment upon himself finally ruined his excellent constitution and, combined with other health problems, made him more and more dependent on alcohol in spite of all his efforts to break away from it. But it must be remembered that in 1946, except for the epileptic fits, the other problems had not taken an acute form. He was full of energy and engaged in arduous creative experiments. In fact, even in his last days, in his broken health, he continued to reinvent himself constantly as an author. In one of

his life. It is true that his dry days should have started from today itself, it is true that he had started last evening by resolving that he would keep it confined to just two pegs and later in honour of the last day had gone on to drink much more. But then he had not known that he would have to go through such experience, that such unthinkable events should unfold before his eyes today, had he? The sound of firing was setting the air and the heart atremble; people were falling to the ground injured or even dead, but still they were unmoved, holding on to the ground. He has been an eyewitness to this terrible nerve-racking drama unfolding on the open stage of the main road, drama that is yet to come to its conclusion, still he cannot believe that such things are really taking place; that the obdurate crowds are even now waiting on the road to find out what would happen next. He is in a state physically and mentally. His head is spinning, let it spin. But suppose on such a day, to mark such an occasion he has a tiny bit to drink, just one or two pegs, how should it matter?

It is now almost eight-thirty in the evening. The drinking bar will close in half an hour. One could still go to a hotel; only it is much more expensive. Suppose he goes quickly, has a fresh peg or two, watches from a safe distance the outcome of events over there and then goes home, what does he have to lose?

If he were to give Alaka[11] detailed accounts of what had happened and explain what a state he had been in, would she not understand? Would she not believe that he had just drunk a bit in this special situation and that otherwise he would have kept his word and not touched the glass? Perhaps he worries unnecessarily; if it is the matter of just a peg or two, may be Alaka would not even

his later letters, he said, 'I am an author, not a drunkard'.

The narrative significance of the fictional situation lies in the emphasis on disruptive elements introduced into middle-class life by the War and the contradictions and the hypocrisy of middle-class respectability exposed in the portrayal of Akshay's domestic relationships.

[11] 'Alaka' inadvertently becomes 'Sudha' later in the narrative.

know. A little drink has no effect on him. Alaka is used to seeing him in a much more fuddled state and would be happy if it does not come to that.

But she might smell it. It could make her retreat from him in sudden aversion and bring that look of pain and worry back to her face as she went rigid with nervousness and agitation. What if she does not calm down even after his explanation?

Just think what his degraded life has come to! Is this the way to approach the unforgettable happenings of today? Shame on him! Shame a hundredfold!

But again, suppose he just takes a drop! When has he ever been in such real need of a drink as now? So far drinking has been just amusement. Today he needs a drop to steady his nerves and stabilise his thoughts. Sometimes people do take a tot as medicine, don't they?

A shooting discomfort keeps Akshay's arteries taut. Like the hand of a clock marking seconds his thoughts go round and round, ascending and descending all the time. Has he ever felt so torn by this simultaneous wild urge and strong aversion within his own self? He has been standing on this little balcony as if for ever. His limbs and his whole body feel stiff from leaning so long on the balustrade. Those who are on the road are sitting in greater comfort than him; of course they are not safe as he is, but are they even concerned about danger? This evening, the road is not lit up as usual by the illumination from the shops. Akshay looks from above in the dim half-light at this particular scene, calm and pregnant with possibilities that might unfold, of today's unforgettable drama and feels a deep churning in his whole being. It is like a cyclonic churning taking place in the unfathomable depths of a sea of melancholy. Can anything match the weary emptiness he experiences? Even as his feelings and thoughts crumble, someone within him seems to whisper tauntingly, these are but the drunkard's games with himself, just one tot can put things right, the useless thoughts fogging your mind can vanish, and then after a few drinks life will be filled with bubbling joy again.

Does he not know himself that his words mean nothing, nor his thoughts and feelings just now? No more than the cloudy vapour of alcohol?

He really does not trust himself.

But people can retain trust in themselves even when facing death. They can die trusting that their death would be useful in some way.

Perhaps without that faith life loses its taste, as his life has. If life loses its taste perhaps all faith also goes, as is the case with him.

How many nights has he spent carousing with his friends, but even in the midst of all that cheer he has remained isolated and companionless. He has only tried to extract his own pleasure from such occasions, desired enjoyment for himself alone, weighed out unsparingly what has been his gain and to what extent he has been outwitted by others. Neither does he feel at one with those sitting on the road, even his thoughts about them are revolving only around his own self.

The praxis is theirs; he is but using it as an excuse for breaking his promise not to drink again. Their glorious challenge to death has merely been appropriated by him to make it an occasion to quench his avidity for celebration. They mean nothing to him, their only value to him being that they have inspired him to philosophise.

'Won't you be leaving now, sir? You really should'.

Makhan's job is to serve as office peon by day and as watchman by night. The big and small officers and all the clerks have left the office long back. This one whose salary is pegged at two hundred rupees is still lingering. What makes him so very afraid of losing his life? All of them went off, even the juniormost clerk with his innocent face, but this one has not ventured downstairs even once from the second floor. Perhaps he intends to spend the night here giving Makhan no end of trouble.

Makhan repeats, 'What are you afraid of, sir? I have myself gone out a couple of times. Don't go that way, just make a detour by the side road and you will reach home safely. Only you will have to walk a bit'.

Akshay says, 'Makhan, it is not that I am afraid of dying'.

'Of course not, sir', Makhan answers humbly. What he cannot imagine is how Akshaybabu is going to have his drinking bout without going outside. Perhaps he carries his own small bottle with him.

'I am just going around a bit, Makhan, you can go to sleep after I come back'.

'You will come back here?'

'Certainly, I will, I shall not be late, just half-an-hour or so'.

Akshay climbs down the stairs. The gatekeeper has locked the front gate. He is surprised to see Akshay and not pleased to hear what he has to say.

'What, coming back?' he says in Hindi.

'Surely I shall come.'

Ram Singh insists that he must keep the gate locked, he cannot leave it ajar. He makes a face in disgust at the babu who has been hiding inside the office in fear and has not mustered courage to return home. He fails to understand the purpose of going out at this hour. No shop selling food or cigarettes would be open now, besides it is the custom that for such needs the gatekeeper may be ordered to fetch and carry. If he was going out at all, why not get back home?

It is difficult to understand the ways of gentlemen, thinks Ram Singh referring back to his long experience of such things.

The main gate opens out into the side road. Akshay moves away in the opposite direction from the place of the happenings. He can reach the drinking bar by making a detour. But it may have already downed its shutters. It is almost nine. Even if it is still open, he would have to gulp down his drink. Then should he go immediately to the hotel? He has little money with him today.

This has been deliberate. He is known to the owner of the bar and may get a drink or two now and pay later. On the other hand, what he has with him in cash would only buy him a peg and a half at a hotel.

Is he then planning to drink a lot?

His own mind intervenes, Let us go to the bar first, have two or three pegs quickly on loan and then spend what you have in cash at the hotel to have a leisurely drink.

It has turned cold tonight. Akshay wraps himself up well in his shawl. Are those people going to spend the whole night on the pavement in this cold? They are going to be frozen. A strong nervous thrill passes through his whole body. He suddenly stops at the big junction of three roads, where special arrangements have been made to keep the street lights blazing. He shakes his head a few times. Had it been three or four years earlier he too might have been sitting all night on the pavement, getting frozen. Even after he got his job for some time his mentality had remained the same. He had come to this pass only in wartime after he found out ways of making extra money on the side.[12]

Akshay recognises Manmohon from their office walking quickly from a distance along the pavement to the east. As Manmohon is about to take the turning towards the office building, Akshay calls him.

Manmohon knows only too well what Akshay is doing here at this time. As they come face to face, he says, 'I am in a hurry, brother!'

'Are you going to the place where the trouble occurred?'

'Yes, I am going there'.

[12] During the World War, various kinds of contractual jobs became means for a section of people to enrich themselves, so that in the city of Calcutta also a class of the newly rich who had no scruples about how they earned and spent their money emerged. Akshay and his drinking companion Rakhal in the narrative are subordinate employees in a bank and make small gains out of commissions given for illicit transactions in which they help.

'When did you hear about it? I did not see you leave the office; I was there too.'

'I had left before lunchtime.'

Manmohon looks at Akshay in a slightly surprised manner, Akshay is speaking quite normally; he does not seem to be the worse for drink.

'What now?' Akshay asks again, 'I suppose you went home in between?'

While speaking, Manmohon keeps on tugging together to his breast the ends of his coat with its buttons undone. Even in the depth of winter Akshay has never seen his coat buttoned up; nor has he witnessed any exception to this habitual gesture.

'No, I had no time. I went to see one of the leaders. Alright then, I am off.'

'Oh oh, I am not drunk, Mohon, don't you see, I have not drunk? You are not going to lose face just by talking to me!'

Manmohon can only hear the suppressed cry of pain in these aggressive words. He feels a bit of sympathy for Akshay, as well as some regret. What low depths you can touch through drunkenness! Sometime back this man had been well, happy and normal. During spare time at the Bank or after office hours how eagerly they had discussed the War, the famine, Independence, the future of peasants and workers; while speaking about long-term problems and the immediate situation, Akshay had revealed the inquisitive and energetic aspect of his mind. But within a short span of time his words had become confused and his sharp eagerness had seemed to grow blunt. See how today his distorted thoughts are quick to imagine insult if someone in pressing hurry wants to take leave, how he gets agitated childishly feeling himself spurned! He even lacks the self-control to keep it to himself.

Manmohon says wishing to pacify him, 'So you have given up drinking?'

'Not quite, but I am trying to.'

Advice would not be of much use; it might not be taken kindly either. So Manmohon says lightly, 'How you manage to do it on your small salary is what I do not understand; I hope you have not run into debt'.

'Not really, I am not a complete fool, I have some savings'.

'I am on my way with an urgent piece of news, I really have to hurry now, do not be offended, brother!' Manmohon does not tarry, he moves on taking long strides.

Akshay is not easy in his mind about Manmohon. Soon after getting this bank job he had formed a very pleasant relationship with the latter. Manmohon has an easy-going and sweet temperament. The fact that no trace of self-importance has been there in his demeanour had initially given the impression that he was mild and timid. But gradually Akshay had come to recognise his inner firmness. His unpretentious behaviour did not signify ineffectuality. It had taken time to learn that Manmohon read a lot and thought deeply about things. He was as disinclined to turn garrulous as to talk about himself.

Manmohon now looks down upon him, shrinks from him. He is sure of that. Others make no secret of it even if they do not put their feelings into words. Manmohon just hides his feelings—that is his sole difference with others. But why should Manmohon pity him? Who wanted his kindness?

These days he suffers from an annoying sense of self-abasement whenever he tries to converse with Manmohon. It leads to all kinds of repercussions.

Akshay feels it is not much use visiting the bar now. What if he had borrowed some money from Manmohon? Manmohon's life is glowing with inner lights; if Akshay had taken money from Manmohon to drown himself deeper in his own darkness would that not be the greatest self-mockery?

Shame on him! Shame a hundredfold!

He crosses the road slowly with reluctant steps. A speeding military vehicle grazes by him; of course, it would have been his own fault if he had got run over. Someone who crosses a main road so carelessly deserves to be run over; that too would have been a form of self-mockery similar to borrowing money from Manmohon. Just at a little distance people had voluntarily faced bullets and died. He might have died while carelessly crossing the road because he had been struck silly after witnessing that!

By now Akshay is standing in front of the bar. Time is almost up and people are coming out in twos and threes. Usually, it is more crowded around this time; this evening obviously many have desisted from coming because transport back would be a problem.

Will he go inside and have done with it once and for all? He can hardly tolerate so much excitement anymore and feels a nervous spasm in his chest.

Or instead of taking that precipitate step which he may not be able to retract later for all the remorse he might feel, should he not perhaps take some time to make up his mind? After all, the hotel will still be open; he may still get something to drink there though in a smaller quantity.

Akshay stops pondering on larger issues at this critical moment. His mind leaves the higher levels of fantasising and touches the ground reality. All he can think of now is that if he goes in and drinks today that would not just be the matter of breaking his promise to Sudha; it would amount to wronging her deeply. She would feel a hundred times more hurt today. On other days, Sudha would expect him to come home drunk, she would not be hoping for something different. But today, even before leaving home he has repeated his promise to Sudha, having drawn her to his breast lovingly. His heart goes out to Sudha. He also feels somehow that to go in now and start drinking would spoil whatever remained pure and untouched in their relationship. After what he has seen on the open road today, that would be sheer villainy.

JUST AT THAT moment Rakhal comes out with tottering steps.

'Ah, so there you are, my hearty! Where have you been all this while?'

'Please, not on the road!' says Akshay, trying to disengage his arm.

'Indeed! So, you are still dry, that's it! Look at me, I have been going on since three,' Rakhal sighs closing his eyes, then peering at him again, 'We must talk, it is urgent! I have been waiting all this while for our Akshaybabu to appear. Shall we go to that Chinese hotel? Let us. We can talk there.'

'I have no money.'

'Money? You are worried about money? How much do you want?'

Rakhal actually draws out a wad of notes from his pocket and starts counting. Failing after two or three tries, he puts the whole lot in Akshay's hands.

'Here, chum, you count. You take your share and give me mine. But I say, chum, don't you try to fool me!'

'What money is this?'

'Oh, indeed I haven't told you yet. That is what I wanted to talk to you about. Chowdhury has given us our commission, as soon as I asked him, he gave the whole amount in cash. Decent fellow! You were worrying about money, now you have got it. Why are we standing here, chum? Let us go. We can share it out after reaching the hotel.'

Before this, Akshay has never seen Rakhal drunk while he was sober himself. They may have met each other in a sober state and then got sozzled together. But even after all their bouts of convivial drinking Akshay has never noticed how Rakhal changes in his drunkenness. There have been many occasions when he had put Rakhal in worse condition than now in a taxi and taken him home. But of course, on those occasions he himself had been a different man too. Is this how he too had behaved? Like Rakhal now?

'You can give me my share tomorrow.'

Rakhal takes the notes from him, lifts his kurta, stashes them in the pocket of the woollen vest underneath and smirks, 'So you have got it badly, eh? You rogue, where did you go on the sly for your drink forgetting your old crony?'

His heart might fail if he spends one minute more with this man, thinks Akshay painfully and turning away walks on with quick strides. From the junction of the three main roads he moves towards his office, stopping in front of the locked gate. For once he has to find out what they are doing.

How to do that? If he climbs to the second floor, he can see only one part of the gathering from a distance; on the other hand, who is to stop him if he walks along the road and finds out what they are doing from close quarters? He might even meet Manmohon there.

Or should he go home?

His heart is quite calm. No more plagued by the deadly whirl of confused devious thoughts on what he should or should not do in every situation, big or small, Akshay finds he can take ordinary normal real decisions for himself very simply. Should he go and sit in the midst of the gathering or get back home—that is the question. The answer is straightforward. There is no need for him to go there and get into trouble; that will do no one any good except satisfy his own whim. It is urgent that he should go home now. That is what he will do.

Still, he cannot leave without finding out for once what they are doing, how they are getting on. He also wants to leave his shawl with them. He will be cold until he gets home; but once he gets back there will be bed and blankets for him for the rest of the night. As for the others they will be spending the night under the open sky. Perhaps his shawl will help to keep warm at least one person there.

IT IS ALREADY past ten in the night; Amrit Majumdar, tired, grim-faced, despondent and outright devastated, gets back home in Ballygunje.[13] It had been a sore trial for him to climb up on the police vehicle to convey Basanta Roy's message to the students; not just that, he had sprained his thigh in getting down. A minor sprain, but now it is hurting nonetheless. The gout in his left leg is also playing up. This kind of gymnastics does not suit him, but the situation in the country is unprecedented. After so many years of familiarity with politics, he is feeling puzzled; he is at a loss to understand which way the tide is about to turn. If it is a meeting in a hall or even a park he can go and make a speech; if struggle is called for he can certainly show he can struggle if a car or a ready-made stage is available. But look at the terrible state to which things have been brought by these people, so that you have to climb on top of a truck to make yourself heard!

Worse, they do not listen to him even after that.

'So, what happened?', asks Mrs. Aruna Majumdar eagerly, 'Did they give you a chance to speak?'

After the whole episode has been recounted to her, Aruna reclines her body, flab artificially reduced to slimness, in deep disappointment on the sofa and bursts out 'You are a nincompoop—you are a clown—you can never do anything right!'

'What can I do? Basantababu never went himself . . .'

Aruna hisses in frustration, 'Did it not dawn on you what a big opportunity Basantababu's absence was for you? How could you not realise that if you had made the effort you could have become a big leader overnight? The stage was left to you, you had no competitor and you turned tail? Oh, you clown! You nincompoop! Never are you going to make anything of yourself!'

'But what could I have done?'

'Do I have to tell you?' Aruna rages on, 'And you have been in

[13] Ballygunje, a locality to the southern extremity of the metropolis, was developing in the 1940s as a fashionable residential area for elite classes.

politics for the last ten years! You understand everything, others take your counsel! If you are given the chance but once, you can swing the country on your little finger! All you can do is boast in front of me, you booby! All the others are against him, that is why he cannot rise, that is why he remains a nobody trailing behind famous people! Blaming others is easy when you yourself lack brains and guts!'

Amrit feels suffocated, the failure of the last ten years hangs heavy in the air. What efforts has he not made, what stratagems has he not adopted, he has even been desperate enough to get arrested and put in jail; and yet all this has neither given him fame, nor charisma, nor the good fortune of being acknowledged as a big leader! Of course, he moves in the company of the leaders, has his say in organisational meetings, even gets a few minutes to appear on the stage and make speeches, sometimes a little more. He buys all the papers next morning and eagerly reads the reports to find out if his name has been mentioned. The search is usually unsuccessful. Even if his name happens to be there, it merely appears in the company of a dozen others.

It is impossible to argue with Aruna, but some self-justification is necessary.

'You are not taking into account the real point, Aruna', says Amrit, 'How could I go against the decision taken by the leaders? Taking initiative on my own would mean defying them, it would have peeved them! Don't you see what a big honour it is that I was sent with the message? How much I am trusted! Such a big responsibility. . . .'

'Where would our leaders be if they did not have obedient followers like you?' This comment from Beena, who has just entered the room hits Amrit harder. She is her mother's daughter. Not having a husband as yet she too practices her sting on her father.

'Shut up, Beena, leave the room', Aruna scolds her. Beena does not obey of course. She knows quite well that this is not a real quarrel; her mother is only trying to goad her father into doing something. She must be in control both of rein and whip and would not have anybody else interfere. So Beena sits quietly at a little distance.

Aruna now discards the heckling tone and says evenly, 'What you have done is the duty of the cadre. Then why are you so aggrieved? You are getting all the respect due to a loyal dutiful party-worker. Why are you so keen on leadership?'

'Who knows?'

'Then let it go, forget about politics, it is not for you! Go and freshen up now!'

Her mildness peeves Amrit. 'What do you mean? You think of me as foolish and ineffectual; then who got you this house? Who got you all this comfort you enjoy—clothes and ornaments and servants galore—who got you all this?'

Aruna turns firmly to Beena and charges on, 'Why did you come home so late? Where have you been all this time?'

Beena does not bother to answer. She knows that her father is being paid back in his own coin. It is not so unusually late that her mother would call for her explanation. This is meant just to reduce Amrit to silence. Amrit lights a cheroot. Perhaps Aruna is giving up and concentrating on domestic life? Perhaps she is no more bothered about his public life? Or does she have something more to say after this?

Bewildered, Amrit repeats his earlier question, 'What would you have me do?'

'Oh, You! You should have realised that the opportunity you had been looking for in the last ten years was facing you. The big ones had stayed away from the trouble and the firing; nobody would interfere with whatever you might say or do. When they refused to accept the message, you should have announced that you were on their side. You should have told them forcefully that you have been serving the country for the last ten or fifteen years, have even been in prison and you stand by your ideals. You should have declared that you were taking full responsibility to make arrangements for a negotiation and you would do it even at the cost of your life . . .'

'What negotiation?' asks Amrit greatly astonished.

'What does it matter? It was for you to say that you took responsibility; if the negotiation did not succeed who was to blame you? You should have talked to them, talked to the police and run around for a while; that was all you had to do. After things settled down and you thought that the people were in the right mood you might have banked on that and come up firmly to claim credit for averting disaster and for making the movement successful with your genuine efforts to get the people's demands fulfilled'.

Amrit sighs and keeps his peace. Not for the first time, he admits to himself that he might have increased his political clout manifold if he had remained in the background himself just promoting his wife as a politician. Even then he would not have been a leader, but he might have been a leader's spouse.

'There is still time'.

Amrit's heart starts palpitating at this low-toned, brief and firm announcement made by Aruna.

Enthusiastically she instructs him, 'Go there again this moment. The leaders are sleeping at home. Go and tell the police that you have come to make peace and to tell the crowd to disperse. Then they will let you speak. But mind you, once you start speaking you must not tell them to disperse. You must start by praising their bravery and telling them that they are the country's future. After that you should make much of all your efforts to get their demands accepted. You must tell them, dear brothers, I missed the privilege of facing police bullets together with you because at that time I was engaged in trying to prevent this alien government from mowing us down with guns. That attempt had seemed to be more important to me at that time. I could not prevent it, so I have come back to be with you in fighting for Independence till death. Speeches you have heard galore; I am not a good speaker, but let us all together . . .'

Aruna stops helplessly in the middle of the sentence. Four hundred million Indians have been listening to her speech so far, but out of nothing, the words 'all together' uttered by her stir up such a terrible reaction within that she sinks as under a deadly blow. No, success will continue to elude her husband. If she has to instruct him from home to make a speech word by word and then if she has to correct herself and tell him that the words 'all together' must not be uttered on any account, how much more can she, a mere woman, do after that?

Beena seems to wake up at last and asks anxiously, 'Ma, what is the matter with you? You are not having that heart pain, are you?'

About one and a half years back, the doctor had given the clear ultimatum that if that pain started again due to neglect in following a normal routine, no doctor in the world would be able to take the responsibility of saving Mrs. Aruna Majumdar from dying of sudden heart failure.

'Oh, nothing is the matter with me! Will you go? Will you be able to utilise this chance? For ten years you have craved for this chance like a beggar, now will you be able to make a success of it? Tell me if you are going!'

'Alright, I am going just now!'

'Beena, tell Halim to get the car out—right now! Even if he is having his dinner tell him to get going; he can have his dinner later! If he refuses, he loses his job from tomorrow! Why don't you go? What have you done in ten years except to get swollen like a balloon? Get to work now!'

'Alright, alright, I am on my way!'

Actually, Halim has not been having his dinner, not just yet. With the days of his youth coming to an end, he too has been worrying about his own problems. He has been driving the car for a long time today—he has no idea how babu manages to get all that petrol though. Since he is hand in glove with big people, he must be having his own ways. On any other day, Halim would have been annoyed if ordered to take out the car after such a hard day; now however he says not a word, but starts off with Amrit at an incredibly high speed.

Meanwhile at Amrit's home Beena goes on calling in anguish, 'Ma, Ma, what is the matter with you? Can you hear me? How are you feeling, Ma?'

The doctor had warned again and again. What was this phantasm that had lured her into complete oblivion of that warning? How this strange madness has impelled her to invoke this death sentence upon herself is all that Beena can think of as she sits with her brothers and sisters watching over her dead mother and waiting for her father to get back. Even in her eating habits, her mother was so disciplined, so how come she had stashed up so much anxiety and frustration within herself? All that she had was not enough; her ambition for fame and power was like a ravaging self-destroying force. She seemed to have gone out of her mind craving to raise her husband to the position of a big leader. What was this terrible fascination for power that her father could not draw away from it even when it filled him with self-disgust and despair; that her mother had to give her life for it! She has committed suicide, thinks Beena. Silent tears run down her cheeks, she cannot weep and wail aloud as her siblings do.

Amrit's thoughts start racing as his car speeds up. He rehearses quickly in his mind what he would say and do, which tricks would yield best fruit. His self-confidence seems to have gone up several notches after a long time and he is quite excited. Aruna is right, it is by being able to utilise such opportunities that one can impress people and turn into a hero. Various possibilities pass through his mind. One plan that particularly excites his avidity and fear at the same time is full of spectacle and drama, something to really stir up people. He can say that he will carry on the movement that has started today; but he can go a step further and announce that in support of their demand and in protest against the firing he is joining them right now—he can join the sit-in. He may be arrested for this; so much the better.

That would make it a big public event. His name would appear in big prints in all the newspapers . . .

But would it? As Amrit sees it, there is a big question mark here. If he goes ahead on his own so drastically, no doubt the big leaders will be peeved. Even an announcement that he would support these people and join their movement would peeve them. If they are peeved no big newspaper will publish his name. If he went further and directly joined the sit-in, they would most certainly see red with anger. It is still not clear what their attitude would be towards today's events, how they would decide to come to terms with them. But Amrit has some idea about what the big ones have in mind. They want to remain detached to the extent possible; they do not wish to give these happenings too much importance. In these days of political dissension, they might even underplay them later as the result of some hot-headed faction or other trying to take credit. That would spell danger for Amrit. He might have to resign from the party or else be forced to sink to the very bottom by retracting his public statement.

Now let us suppose, calculates Amrit to his own mind, trying his best to keep his cool, such a thing happens and he is discarded by the leaders, would there not be still some gains? Will there not be some public uproar around his move? Perhaps he can make his way upwards by joining some other party. For such a long time, he has waited upon the leaders without result; how about moving on in a different direction? But on the other hand, suppose that chance never came. Suppose his political strategy falls through? Then he is sure to lose both ways.

If he makes the more moderate announcement and gets back home, whatever the outcome he will be able to outlive it. But it will not have the same effect as the more extreme course he is thinking of—that step might even make him a hero overnight. Amrit dithers. He regrets not having Aruna at his side to counsel him; her presence might have helped him to reach a decision.

The car moves through a side road and stops close to the

turning. The crowd has thinned out somewhat. As Amrit gets down and starts walking a rather tall young man in a coat with the buttons undone comes up to meet him.

'I have something to tell you, sir'.

'I can't quite . . .'

'Oh, I am not someone you know. Your wife is suddenly very ill. You must get back home directly. Subrato came here after getting a phone call from your home, your daughter was calling. Subrato has gone there after telling us to inform you'.

'She is ill! What is the matter with her? But now I have come here . . .'

Manmohon wonders at Amrit's reluctance and hesitation. Perhaps he has not been able to understand the gravity of the situation from his words? He says again, 'I heard she has had a heart attack; her condition is very serious. You have to go right now'.

A heart attack could be fatal for Aruna. Of course, she had seemed alright when he left, but on the other hand, a heart attack can turn critical within minutes. But how to manage the situation here? This is not the time to take the extreme step he has been mulling on, so it is better to make his speech and get back home as soon as possible. In fact, he might even add that his heart is with them and he is only going away leaving them in this state because his wife is seriously ill. . . .

'I have come here to tell all of you something. Let me have ten minutes and then I shall go home'.

'Is it some announcement from your party?'

'Not exactly, it is something I want to say on my own. Now we have to build up a big movement all over the country, I want to say on my behalf that I pledge to join you with all my strength to do this'.

Manmohon's heart sags with exhaustion as he hears this. But maintaining his serious tone with great patience he replies, 'Do you think it will be appropriate? No one is prepared for a speech right now. There is to be a meeting in the morning, it is better to wait for that if you want to speak.'

'Then you will not allow me to speak?'

'There is no question of stopping you if you want to speak. But please consider whether you should. Our morale is strong. At most some people will feel a bit more boosted by your speech. It will be much more effective if you tell the public what you want to tell in the morning'.

The excitement and eagerness felt when he had left home and while he was in the car is ebbing out. The situation is quite calm now, but in the light of the confrontation that has taken place here between armed aggression and unarmed resistance Amrit finds it utterly unfamiliar and beyond comprehension. He feels this does not fit with anything in his experience over all these years. The rules of the game that are known to him have not worked here. It would be most difficult—perhaps impossible—for him to cope with this.

He returns to his car—Amrit, the undying one—feeling as if he is dead.

'Halim, speed up!'

His head spins and winking stars dance in front of his eyes.

AJOY KEEPS HIS distance and watches it all as if he is not interested. No, he has no complaints, but much to dishearten him. His nineteen-year-old heart is harrowed by a sense of grievance.

Those people had come out in a rally and after being stalled in their progress are now sitting on the road. This novelty of being on the road together makes them bubble over with excitement. Turmoil will continue over the events; celebrities will rush to and fro communicating with the higher authorities and there will be negotiations galore until the matter is resolved through an understanding. Then they will all go home preening themselves, narrating to their family and their neighbours, and their girl-friends and acquaintances at boarding-houses, hostels and tea-shops the story of their struggle. If it had happened eight months back, he too might have been here as one of them, gone home and narrated to the wide-eyed Madhu the account of their struggle.

But today he is not one of them anymore. He is no longer a college student. Not for him that carefree season of dreams, aspirations and exultation even in the midst of want and distress. The ecstasy of ignoring the challenge of batons and bullets and sitting down on the road when prevented from rallying ahead is a thing of the past for him. He is now a clerk, a man with a job. His monthly salary of forty rupees is all his pleasure, all his hope and all his future. The limits of his life for all time to come have been defined by the tin roof, the mud walls and the red cement floor of the rooms he occupies in a house in an old shabby-genteel neighbourhood of Howrah, next to the bustee. His unlaundered clothes and the cheap faded shawl he carries around his body are the insignia of what he is for all time to come.

There are many like him in the gathering, ordinary passers-by. Even that youth whom he has seen packing beedis in the shop in front of his office for the last few months, is here. But still Ajoy continues to feel aggrieved. The passers-by are of course here from curiosity. To go and join them would make him just another inquisitive by-stander. Even if he announces that he had himself been a student a few months back, they would not regard him as one of them. Now that he is a student no more, he does not belong. He has no right to be with them.

He wants a beedi for a smoke.[14] He does not have one and must buy.

[14] There is a class difference between the cigarette and the beedi; the latter consisting of a rolled dry leaf from the sal tree with tobacco packed in by hand. It is cheaper than the cheapest cigarette and favoured by working class smokers. For a man with a white-collar job or even a student, smoking a beedi would signify going down in the world.

He could get a cigarette or two from his friends earlier. He only had to buy a couple over and above and make it last. After he got the job, he had started buying five cigarettes every day with his own money, cheap cigarettes of course, five for just two annas; you could get a pack of beedis for the same amount. Then he had to give it up. To save money on public transport he has to walk every day from the bridge right up to his office. How can he afford to smoke cigarettes? Then he took to beedis, but gave up in disgust. His craving is for cigarettes, but not having the wherewithal must he make do with beedis? Better to go without smoking then!

Madhu said when she heard this, 'Don't you wish to live in a house like the latsahib's?'[15]

'Certainly not!'

'Don't lie!'

It is strange that Madhu does not understand the difference between a craving and a dream. To have a bellyful of rice is a craving while having delicious pulau is a dream. She should understand that since she is already hankering after some way to earn some money.

Look at that man, smoke rising from the cigarette held between his fingers. He seems to be too lazy even to take a pull. Laziness is evident in the manner of his standing too. He has stopped on his way to find out what the matter is, but it looks like he could not care less. From the pocket of his fine kurta the colourful cigarette container is showing.

No harm in buying just one beedi for this once His resolve is not to smoke a single cigarette until he can earn enough to satisfy his craving; after all he has not taken a vow not to have a single beedi in the meantime. He feels dreadful standing apart from them like an untouchable. Maybe he will feel a little better after a smoke.

He has not had a beedi for the last five days. It has been quite a

[15] Derived from the word 'lord', 'latsahib' refers to the governor of the province of Bengal under colonial rule. It is his palatial mansion that Madhu is ironically referring to.

trial and he is still feeling deprived. The craving is still quite strong, but is it worth spoiling the effort of the last five days just to have one smoke now? Is it that essential?

'Babu! Babu! Please listen! Can you tell us how to get to Sealdah?'

How strange, thinks Ajoy. Do all the bumpkins from the countryside newly-arrived at the city and feeling at a loose end wait agape for Ajoybabu to turn up like a saviour and direct them to their true destination? Respectable gentlemen desiring information always avoid him and seek others to answer their query; but people of this sort somehow turn away from others to seek his help. Does he look like one of them, like a village bumpkin, that they seek succour from him as from someone of the same breed? Accompanied by a very young bride all covered up and an older woman, this man has been waiting on the pavement of one of the side roads looking this way and that, now staring at one face and now at another. Finally avoiding all the passers-by in between, he reaches Ajoy and stands facing him.

'You have to make a detour to get there', says Ajoy and gives him the direction and tells him how to reach the place. But the man scratches his head and looks quite at sea.

'Come with me!'

Ajoy takes them along the side road and having reached the turning calls a rickshaw and puts them on it. Then he stands hesitating a bit as if he is not sure which way to go. Should he go home or turn back where the gathering is? He is not one of them. Their path is not his path.

He feels a strong desire to go back there, to see what they do and to learn how the confrontation would culminate. Even as an outsider he can wait and watch their activities; he is not going to demand a place in their midst just because only eight months back he has lost the stamp of identity they still have.

Just then he hears the rat-tat-tat of guns and the terrible

tumult of voices reaches his ears. He forgets everything, all his grudge and discontent turn into one overwhelming question: What is this? What is this? Frightened people rush past him in the opposite direction, he hardly glances at them. Rather he is aware of a strange exhilaration that their numbers are small. A few maybe turning back in fear, he must see what the others are doing.

He forgets that he has been standing apart as a mere spectator and runs right into their midst.

IT IS PAST midnight in Madhukhali. The misty darkness in the eastern part of the village is tinged blood-red by tongues of fire. The river is also tinged red as if it has been touched by the rising sun. The house of Keshab, the village physician, is about a mile further towards the sea. Even from here, the fires of Madhukhali are visible.

Jadav keeps on groaning in pain as he says, 'Why don't you lie down for a while, Ganesh's mother? Rani, get some rest, my dear! Who knows how much more trouble fate has in store for us?'

'What is the use of lying down? They may call us and put us on our way before we have time to close our eyes! If it is our fate to suffer, we have to suffer!' Ganesh's mother yawns widely and even as she yawns adjusts the covers under which the two younger children have fallen asleep almost as soon as they got a place to sleep in.

Rani holds up the thatch covering the window and continues to stare at the signs in red in the distance. She seems not to have even heard Jadav's plea for her to take rest. The fibres of her body are so weary that they crave to fall heavily on the ground to seek rest; her knees may even give in at any moment. Still she feels powerless to turn her eyes away from those red signals of fire. It is not just that some prettily thatched cottages with white-washed mud-walls are burning away there—the gods had lit those flames as in Seeta's fire-trial at the last moment to protect her innocence.[16] She had only heard a tremendous uproar replacing the low singing in her ears and she had thought her ear-drums would burst cracking her skull and causing her brains to spill: this is my moment of death, she had thought. Once dead, it would not matter what that fat short fellow did with her body; at least her senses would be spared all that. Did she have any idea that the whole village would turn out to rescue her from her abductor, that Ravana? It had been beyond her belief; she had only thought that it was the roar of the tidal bore entering the river.

Was the man burning in that fire? Even in that same long dressing-gown he had put on after undressing himself and telling her 'nothing to fear' 'nothing to fear' all the time? Rani takes a deep breath, as if the smell of burning flesh can reach her at such a distance. She remembers seeing as she came out of the room that some people were beating up that fellow in a frenzied manner. Was he finished off and left to burn with the house? Or did they tie him up with the bedstead alive before setting the house on fire? She wishes she had slipped out and bolted the door behind her and called the others to make sure that he was burnt alive and squealing.

The sharp night air touches her face, but she does not feel cold. All her other senses dead, she is only conscious of the heat of the pyre on which her tormentor was set aflame.

Ganesh's mother advices Jadav, 'Instead of shivering with cold there and telling us ten times to lie down, why don't you come this side and stretch out under the cover yourself?'

'What! Is this the time for me to lie down?'

[16] Rani was abducted to the police camp or barrack set up in the village on the pretext of keeping law and order at a time when, as the narrative tells us, discontent had been running high among the peasantry in the area. The allusion to the mythological trial by fire has a twist in it because in the Ramayana, Seeta's fire-trial was not to protect her chastity from her abductor but to prove her chastity to her rescuers.

His wife presses her thin fist against her mouth suppressing her uncontrollable yawns and says, 'Just sitting up like this you cannot solve the problem. If we can once reach the city where our son is, what do we have to fear? These people are doing everything to help us to get there'.

Jadav is silent.

'You are not alone. Much could you do to save our daughter by yourself; all that is empty boast! Other people have wives and daughters. They saw that if they allowed this kind of thing to go on no one would be safe; that is why they rushed together in desperation. Their anger was simmering over what had happened during harvest time—that is what turned into a blessing for us. They rescued our girl and set fire to the camp; then they shifted us here the same night, they will surely be able to send us to the city. It is for you to be a little more active now, but all you do is to sit cowering in fear and worry!'

The flame of the kerosene lamp keeps on flickering in the sharp wind from the north. Looking at his wife's meagre and worn body, Jadav is reminded of the swing of scraggy jointed bamboo trees. The storm that whisks away the straw roof of peasant huts and fells giant trees without effort can only make the bamboo tree swing unconcernedly to and fro. Ganesh's mother is bent down under the calamities of life, but continues with her own convictions in her own way. Otherwise, how can she talk so smoothly to persuade him to take some rest under the cover when such terrible disasters have overtaken them and when they are waiting under the roof of other people to start on their uncertain city-ward journey? Ganesh's mother is quite content to make some kind of general sense out of all this. Her daughter had been forcibly abducted and taken to the police barracks. The villagers had seen red and rushed out to rescue her immediately. They had also set fire to the barracks. Then they had helped her family to flee the village overnight and are making arrangements to send them to the city where Ganesh is. After having learnt all this Ganesh's mother has stopped weeping and worrying. She is quite unaware of the troubles that lie ahead. She could not be bothered about where all this turmoil would culminate, why they were being spirited away in such a hush-hush manner, what further disasters they might have to encounter in the coming days. She is just happy to think that they are going to be with their son in the city—the son who is now on a job and sending them money every month.

Rani says suddenly her face still turned towards the window, 'Dad, the fire is still burning, see, it is burning on!'

Ganesh's mother says in a cool voice, 'You could have lain down a little, Rani!' She bears no grudge against the girl although she knows that it is because of her that they are in this peril. It is alright to blame her for being a girl in the context of ordinary day-to-day domestic irritants. But how can she be made responsible for this terrible out-of-the-way calamity? Ganesh's mother suffers from a different kind of worry. Her daughter has not been violated, but will people accept it? They may not actually say it, they may even be sympathetic, but the mark of having been defiled will still be stamped on her in the eyes of people. Perhaps her son-in-law Sudhir will make it an excuse to desert her. Will Rani be able to endure all that? What will she do if it becomes unendurable? She is reminded of an earlier incident when the adolescent daughter of Podi had been abducted and taken to the police camp in Santra. All night Podi had gone round and round the camp wildly with her daughter's helpless wailing in her ears. When she came back to the village in the morning with her half-dead daughter, what uproar had broken out! All the peasantry, both Hindus and Muslims, had been up in arms and if the magistrate had not visited the village himself and promised justice, there would have been a big outbreak. That outbreak finally occurred in her daughter's case. Everyone had supported Podi's daughter, they had been sympathetic with all their hearts; she had herself broken into tears once when she held the girl in her embrace and uttered a few words of comfort. Still Podi's daughter drowned herself in the village pond. What would

Rani have done if they had stayed back? Perhaps this is better for her. Their small house and landholding are heavily mortgaged on account of debt. What should they stay back for? Better to go to the city where among unknown people Rani would be able to live undisturbed and they too would find peace.

For Ganesh's mother the dream of peace and happiness resides mostly in the outward shell of life. She cannot remember ever having asked for more, nor does she dare to. How happy and peaceful she would feel only if she does not have to die of hunger, only if she is not brought to death's door by disease or some calamity of that kind, only if she has some kind of a roof over her head!

Keshab comes in carrying an old blanket, having covered himself in a home-made wrapper. His manners are easy and mild, with a touch of gravity. He does not seem to be particularly agitated at the prospect of entertaining this family that have become his guests completely out of the blue.

He puts the blanket down next to Jadav and says in a congenial voice, 'Khichri is almost ready, rest a little after taking food as you must start soon. You can have a snooze in the boat; they are looking for a boat.'

'All of you are in danger because of me. I don't feel like running away, doctor sir!'

Keshab nods his head as if he understands the feeling: 'But you are not running away, why should you? The point is that they are not going to leave us just like that; there is going to be mayhem for the next few days. You are the immediate target and are going to be hit first. So you have to stay safe for a few days. As things turn better and people protest more and more they will refrain from their lawless attacks. When legal enquiry starts', continues Keshab with a hint of a smile on his face, 'You will have to come back and give witness. Your daughter will be the principal witness.'

'I have to give witness? I shall. Indeed, I shall give witness', says Rani, moving away from the window at last.

Keshab nods his head in confirmation.

Jadav asks a little doubtfully, 'Can't we stay in hiding somewhere near?'

'Were you not saying that you can go to your son? Perhaps that is better; go to Kolkata', says Keshab, stroking his beard thoughtfully, 'Who knows whether there will be the opportunity to give witness! Landlord Jagatbabu will not miss this chance to take it out on his difficult tenants. One cannot be sure what counsel he will offer, what kind of a twist he will give to all this! No, I think it is better for you to go to your son'.

Keshab's wife Menaka enters without ceremony and calls them to come and have their food. She says, 'Bring that kerosene lamp with you, my dear, what is your name? Rani, is it? Oh dear, look, the lamp is burning out!'

Keshab says, 'There is no more kerosene'.

'Never mind; let me pour out a little from the kitchen lamp!'

Menaka makes all of them sit together and have their food, even Ganesh's mother and Rani. As he raises the khichri to his mouth, Jadav's eyes suddenly brim with tears. From the outset he has been overwhelmed by this experience that even the life of a poor nobody like him is precious to others, that his daughter's honour matters to them as much as that of their own daughters. He has always known that he is quite without help. During the famine he has felt in his bones that it does not matter in the slightest to anybody whether his family lives or dies. But today he knows that is not true. His right arm has been injured so that he finds it difficult to put food in his mouth, the wound on his head under the bandage is hurting; but all that hardly worries him. Rather it is the sense of anger and unrest within him which is being strongly aroused even by the physical pain. He is going to return. He will leave his wife and children with Ganesh and come back to those who are fighting here.

The struggle against depriving sharecroppers of their portion and against forced labour had been getting stronger in the village by the day. It was the trouble that had been brewing over these that had encouraged the men from the barracks to drag away his daughter even before evening had fallen. Jadav regrets that at that time he had not really joined that struggle seriously. How could he have been indifferent to it when people involved in it saw him as one of their own and came out to help him defying danger and death?

Even before they finish eating, the two who had gone in search of a boat are back.

Within half-an-hour, the boat starts off with them. Rani sits outside facing the red glow of the fire, nobody can stop her. The boat will cross Madhukhali on its way.

SOMEONE WHO IS already dead, someone in particular who looks as if he is a mere day-labourer does not give the staff at the hospital much of a headache. It is as if his relatives too might be somewhat less interested in learning about his death, as if the lifeless body is somewhat less precious to them. For sure, the main responsibility of the hospital is over with the patient's death. It is those living who concern them more. Osman is aware of that. Apart from that, the sudden arrival of a large number of injured, many of them in critical condition, is creating a lot of work for the staff. Even then, can nobody afford a moment to open the package wrapped up in gunny cloth and find some way of establishing the identity of the dead? If some information can be had, Osman is ready to walk any distance to make enquiries. But that move has been postponed till tomorrow. No use making trouble. Everybody is too busy.

In Ganesh's breast pocket a piece of paper with an address written in English was found. The address was of one L. Cameron of James Street. After a great deal of persuasion Osman had been able to get someone to call there. But Cameron said he had no idea what the package was. He had not ordered any package and no package was to be received by him.

Not much use standing here; it was late night now. He would come again tomorrow to see if there was something to be done. Osman felt as if he was leaving a blood-relative here, one about whom he knew nothing. There were slight signs of life in his body when they were on their way to the hospital, even if these were not evident from the outside. But then that thin flow of life had ebbed out silently. The boy's real miraculous death had taken place on the road, in his close proximity, when with the bullet in his brain he had still kept standing, still kept talking until he went down of a sudden, insensible and unresponsive. Not a single moan had escaped his lips. He had shown not a single sign of his fatal injury; but impatient and anxious he had persisted in his last question: 'Are they not going to move on?' Even then Osman had not known that the boy's life was coming to an end, that never more would he have the opportunity of enquiring when the people checked in their advance would move forward again. Perhaps the bullet had paralysed a part of his brain and had caused him to react that way. That is what the young doctor had explained to him as a possibility; Osman does not care what it was. His whole consciousness is overwhelmed by the death. He may forget his closest relatives; but this boy by his strange death would live in his mind forever. Till the day of his own death, he is not going to forget that urgent question: 'Are they not going to move?'

On the way out he meets Rasul and Sibnath. Rasul's right hand is bandaged, his face pale from loss of blood. Sibnath is scolding him for having wasted so much time losing blood all the while.

Osman recognises them, but he feels a little doubtful about addressing them on his own initiative. These two were his son's friends and had known him as Habib's father.[17] They knew him as

[17] Osman's son Habib was evidently a friend and contemporary of Rasul and the others. Here we are not told how he died, but it is obvious that he had been a mentor to Rasul whose illusions about upper class leaders he had known and sought to correct. But later in the narrative when Amina recalls the story of his son's death as told by Osman himself there is a shift in the relationship between Rasul and Osman's son. It is the latter who suffers from illusions about high-ups from his own community and pays for it with his

a tram conductor. His son is no more. He is in the garb of a factory worker. If he goes and talks to them there are bound to be some clumsy exchanges; why go in for an uncomfortable conversation? It may not matter to Osman, but why embarrass them?

But Sibnath recognises him too and is the first to ask, 'You here?'

Rasul in his weak voice also asks, 'Why are you here, sahib? Is there someone you know . . .'

'I brought a boy with a bullet in his head. He died.' A little hesitantly Osman adds, 'No, not anyone I knew. He was standing near me. Then suddenly . . .'

'You will find it difficult to get back home.'

'I can walk.'

'That of course.'

Osman seems already to know what has happened to Rasul's arm and asks 'Is it possible to save that arm?'

'I do not know; it is doubtful.'

'It is the right arm too!'

The three of them walk together, their hearts heavy with the thought of all the afflictions, injuries, pain, deaths, suffering and despair which inhabit the hospital area. Still, they go along speaking easily as if living persons have no call to be unnecessarily agitated or troubled by the unreasonable curses of life.

Rasul has been more-or-less silent. He suddenly stops and turns to Sibnath 'I am ashamed to tell you, brother, but I think I am about to faint . . .'.

Osman and Sibnath take hold of him from either side and ease him down gently on the ground. Osman kneels down and makes Rasul lean against him head reclining on his chest.

'What an idiot you are, Rasul!' Says Sibnath as he puts his shawl around Rasul.

life admitting his mistake to his father before his death. This is one more example of authorial inadvertence in the novel.

Osman adds, 'A rare idiot indeed! He had thought he would get home without troubling anyone. Habib used to say, Rasul feels ashamed of falling ill!'

'That is why everyone is so fond of the fellow!'

Rasul says apologetically, 'I did not realise I had lost so much blood. If I had I would not have waited for an instant, I would have come here at once'.

Rasul is admitted to the hospital. When Osman and Sibnath come out on the road, the deserted silence all around makes the deep night almost tangible.

Sibnath is always calm and cool, completely without airs. No one has known him to have ever lost his sense of proportion; he seems to be able in a moment to gauge what is coming from what is happening right now and act accordingly—whether it is some small chore or some really big task. There is no work that he minds doing, from speaking in a meeting to acting as a courier, just as now he has taken it upon himself to reach Rasul to the hospital. Whatever task you set him, he will do it with all his heart; but he is not happy doing the same kind of work all the while. While the action was going on, he had taken the role of leadership quite effortlessly; now that he is not needed there anymore, he has assumed the different responsibility of getting the injured Rasul hospitalised. Maybe when he gets back he will make arrangements to get tea for those who are sitting on the road under the open sky and suffering the biting cold.

No, that is not what Sibnath is going to do now, thinks Osman a bit awkwardly, Sibnath will do no such out-of-the-way thing. He will do only what is needed for the occasion. Osman is unable to guess what that may be.

It is Rasul from whom he has learned about Sibnath. He has an unusual capacity to adjust himself in any situation at any time, even with regard to his family. His seniors there do not find at all congenial all this work he does outside home, but within the family they always act according to his advice, whether the matter is marriage or medical treatment for someone.

When Sibnath begins to talk Osman has to admit it, yes, this boy is really of that mettle. This is a night replete with strange events; one would have thought that it would be proper to walk along in silence. There are people lying on the pavement bundled up in rags; mangy dogs are also lying curled up in front of the shuttered butcher's shop. It was really not expected that Sibnath should say something. But as soon as he speaks Osman feels that it would have been a deprivation if Sibnath had merely walked with him in total silence.

'A boy like Rasul is difficult to find. His right arm is as likely as lost, but he is already thinking how he can manage to do all the work he is doing now with his remaining arm. Rasul is like a brother to me!'

How appropriate are Sibnath's words and how they tally with the very thoughts that are in Osman's mind! How did Sibnath know how keenly he had wanted to say something of this sort?

Osman says, 'Rasul is like a son to me!'

Sibnath keeps quiet waiting to understand the direction Osman's words are taking..

Osman says, 'He is most genuine. But he had one defect. He thought that the high-up ones would understand the sorrows of the poor, that they would turn the world into paradise for them. He would always have arguments with Habib on this. I listened to all that when I was there. One day I told Habib, what is the use of having this war of words with someone who would not understand! But Habib said he is all genuine within. One day he is sure to understand; if such people do not understand and change, who will?'

Walking on in silence now, Osman thinks, Rasul has changed. This is Habib's doing. Habib would have been glad if he had been alive. But Habib lives in this boy. So Rasul seems to be like a son to him.

ANURUPA DOES NOT appear to be worrying in the least as she sits chatting with the others. She wears her gentle smile on her face, but a slight sense of discomfort does not leave her. Why is not Hemanta back? It is already two on the wall-clock. He always returns home straight after college. He tells her ahead of time if there is any possibility of delay; otherwise he visits home once before going out again. Also, classes have been disrupted today. Hemanta's is a government college. Even if lectures did take place, he should have been home long before this.

In another half-hour she would have to go out to give tuitions in music. Will he not come back before that?

She gets tea from the tea-shop next door for her guests and says apologetically, 'I have run out of sugar, so I had to give you ready-made tea from the shop.'

'It really does not matter.'

'We are all in the same condition. When I have guests, I too get tea from a shop. What to do? What we get is not even enough for ourselves.'

'I get some extra sugar. It costs a rupee for a seer. But what else is there to do? You cannot do without sugar. There is a shop in our locality from where we get both sugar and cooking oil. The shopkeeper only sells these to people who are known to him. Of course, he fears to do otherwise.'

'I get some sugar too, I buy half a seer two or three times early in the month and store it up, they give only a small amount at a time. You get it for a rupee per seer? I am charged four annas more.'[18]

Anurupa says, 'That way you can buy it of course, but I do not do that. I feel bad about it because it means encouraging the black market; besides if my eldest gets to know about it . . .'

[18] This refers to the rationing of essential goods and the black market which also thrived even after the War was over. The decimal system was yet unknown. Four annas is a quarter of a rupee. A seer is an amount slightly less than one kilogramme.

Anurupa regrets immediately having made this absent-minded remark while thinking about her son. She can see two faces looking ill-pleased at her words. But she also has a happy thought and brushes her regret aside: what is done cannot be undone, but Hemanta will enjoy the story, he will feel pleased with it. She will narrate it properly while serving him dinner.

'Who knows when the situation is going to improve?'

'Telling me? After the War, one hoped things would be better. Still no respite; we are going from bad to worse! My husband's brother is about to lose his job. He expects us then to support his whole family. For the last three years they had been on their own; I might have saved some money, but that was impossible while the War was going on. My husband was humming and hawing, but I made him write back saying clearly that we cannot possibly support them in such hard times. Tell me, is it at all possible?'

'My second and third sons have already got redundancy notices. My mind has stopped working. My eldest is on his own; he lives in Delhi and hardly answers our letters!'

The fear and despondency that hover in the atmosphere like stagnant mist roll into the room in the course of this subdued conversation like a breath of gentle wind. Anurupa swallows hard. Her throat is dry and itching a little. Suppose something happens to her so that she loses her voice before Hemanta can complete his studies and take responsibility! Such things do happen to singers. Giving singing lessons is a troublesome job; so much strain on one's voice morning, day and night! She might give up one or two tuitions, but then how would she run her household and pay for Hemanta's education?

'Why don't you sing a song for us?'

'Song?' Anurupa comes out with her gentle smile, 'My voice is gone; giving music lessons has spoilt it for me! I really cannot sing these days.'

So, a bit turned off, the guests take leave. Anurupa knows what they think. They think she is proud because she has a little talent, because she has made a name. What would they know of her fears about exercising her voice any more than she absolutely has to?

Jayanta says, 'Ma, can I go out and play?'

'Why, what were you doing all this while?'

Anurupa knows it is no use asking. This boy just would not leave the room when guests are there. A thirteen-year-old lad, what does he find to attract him in the conversations of elderly women?

'Go, but do not go far. Come back early'.

Rama has gone to visit Shanta. She has promised to practice her newly-learned song after coming home. Anurupa will check on her own daughter's music lesson after she finishes her rounds teaching music to other peoples' daughters. Anyway, Rama need not give too much effort to her singing lessons. Whatever she learns would be enough for her. Her talent is limited and even if she is tutored well, she will not be able to make much headway. Anurupa sighs. In the empty house all of a sudden, she feels tired and worn-out. This inertia might have disappeared if Hemanta had come. She would have then recovered the energy to go out and teach music to young girls who do not even have sufficient sense of music to recite a nursery rhyme, or who are so charmed by the sound of their own voices that they hardly notice how out of tune they are.

At such times, when the children are not there, Anurupa's heart is heavy with the shadow of indefinable anxieties. To ensure safety she has drawn narrow limits around her life and dispensed with everything except the minimum needed to ensure peace and bring up her children properly. Even after she has achieved all this, from where do all these signs of disturbance and disaster keep on appearing? Why does the heart go bounding within her timid breast? She had hardly felt so disturbed by the World War. It did hit her household, but all she had to do was to scrimp and scrounge to survive. Even the days of bombing had not distressed her that much. Those were distant dangers not likely to touch the little nest with its four inhabitants. But now the menace could be felt like the calm before a storm or the gathering of dark clouds in the firmament over one's head. When one reads newspapers the rumble of a tremendous mass anger can be felt between the lines. Street conversations give a hint of the thoughts of the masses seeking a direction; there are meetings and rallies everywhere which express these thoughts in the roar of thousands of voices. Is it possible to keep intact the harmony within the domestic sphere when the mind is all the time being agitated by events which are involved with the very foundations of life?

Rama comes back in great excitement.

'So, you did not go out? You did quite right. The trams are not running, mother, did you know? Serious troubles have broken out; they are saying that there has been firing. . . . What are you thinking of, Ma?'

'Nothing. Only Hema is not home yet.'

'Oh, you are worried about Dada?' Says Rama lightly, 'Dada is not one to get involved ever in such things. Must have gone somewhere, will be back soon. You don't have to worry for him.'

Rama's tone grates on Anurupa's ears. She is worried that Rama's words might carry a slight hint of contempt about her elder brother.

'I am not worrying,' she says, 'Would you like to practice that song, Rama? Then change your clothes and come!'

Rama however looks most reluctant.

'Leave it today, Ma. Who wants to practice songs today?'

'Then let it be.'

Jayanta returns even more excited. He narrates to Anurupa everything he has learnt from his trip outside. He proposes something quite dangerous.

'Can I just go and have a look, Ma? Just for a moment. I shall only watch from a distance and come back. Can I go?'

'No'.

'Why? What is wrong with just going for a minute? I shall come back and do my homework'.

'You don't have to do your homework today. Go wash your face and hands. Then I shall tell you a story'.

'I don't like made up stories'.

He does not like made up stories! Even this young boy is asking for a story about tangible concrete things!

THE NIGHT WEARS on, but Hemanta is still not home. Anurupa waits with bated breath for the knock on the front door. Her uneasiness has long peaked into anxiety. Even Rama is worried.

After Jayanta falls asleep Anurupa says, 'Let me go and look for him, Rama'.

'Where will you go so late?'

'Let me go to Seeta. They have a telephone at home'.

SEETA HAD ONLY just returned. After Hemanta left, she too had got ready and gone out. Although she had been upset that had not caused her to go off food and she had had a full meal. But since that time, she has been unable to get a breather, not to speak of finding something to eat. Now however she feels no craving for food at all. The sight of known and unknown friends dying around her has set her mind in turmoil. This is different from poetic feelings of personal sorrow. She feels nothing but fury now. It has been burning within her strengthening her will.

'Hemanta? He is not home yet?'

At the meeting she had had a brief glimpse of him. His presence had meant little to her. Rather she had surmised that perhaps he had turned up to find more material for his wrangle with her. After that, he has not even been in her mind; neither did she have the leisure nor the inclination. It is painful for her to conclude once and for all that there is no hope that Hemanta might change. On any other day this would have continued to disturb her, and she would have to get adjusted to the thought by reflecting on that pain and disappointment. But today all thought about such personal matters has left her altogether; that sort of pain and disappointment seems to have receded to the distance.

She feels hardly any sympathy for Anurupa. As she sees it, it would be dishonest to sympathise with this distorted articulation of motherliness. She is a little surprised that Anurupa's anxiety is not expressed on her face, but then to come searching dementedly for a grown-up son just because he has not reached home by early evening is itself sufficient indication of it. How many mothers today have sent their sons to face police bullets while waiting steadfastly at home themselves! And look at this lady who feels that the world has come to an end just because her son has not come home after his evening relaxation! Perhaps this is what makes Hemanta so self-centred, the fact that he is thoroughly spoilt!

Seeta says with an unconcerned air, 'He must have gone somewhere, he is sure to come back after a while'.

'But have you not met him?'

'He came here once in the morning, around twelve or so'.

Anurupa has come to her searching for her lost son. Why to her when there are hundreds of other people? At last, it dawns on Seeta. So she has a place in the dreams dreamt by mother and son about their happy and prosperous future. Seeta could have laughed outright. Anurupa knows or at least surmises that one day Seeta will marry Hemanta and become a part of the family. By reading her son's mind she has guessed that this girl is to his liking and she has not lost time in drawing conclusions from that. After all her son has so much merit and such a brilliant future in front of him that it has not even crossed her mind what Seeta's feelings in the matter may be.

Now Seeta understands why Anurupa is hiding the signs of her worry. She is behaving typically like the future mother-in-law with her future daughter-in-law. Seeta must be distraught with anxiety, so she thinks; she must not disturb her further but it should rather be her role to give her courage.

Hence Anurupa is somewhat perplexed and hurt by Seeta's air of unconcern.

'He is never late without telling me, Seeta! I can't understand what the matter is'.

Seeta feels like laughing, but not a sign shows on her face. The sense of absurdity is quickly replaced by sadness. She can now look into the heart of Hemanta's blind preconceptions. He is not to be blamed. Brought up under the vigilant eyes of such a mother from his very childhood how can he help his weaknesses? Seeta knows that the shape the mind takes in childhood can hardly change later. Only a conscious and uncompromising struggle at a later stage can make a person's feelings and ideas take a new direction. What is more difficult in human life than this struggle against oneself? Suppose you choose your own path by exercising your intellect, but following it in one's action can become a burden if one's nature opposes it. Intellectualism finds its nemesis here. It is so much easier to be driven by one's blind passions and desires than to work out in practice the consequences of decisions taken intellectually. This is why intellectuals so often fail, that they lack conviction so severely, that their frustration expresses itself in mere wordiness.

Seeta says severely, 'Auntie, your son is not a baby'.

'You do not understand me. I am worried that he may have got involved in some trouble, something may have happened to him'.

Seeta's laughter is bitter this time, 'Hemanta is not one to get involved in trouble; so do not worry'.

Anurupa, hurt in her mother's pride, insists: 'What a thing to say! It might have made some sense a year back; but do you want to tell me that you have not noticed how Hema has been changing in the last few months? How can I believe you? A new restlessness has come over him; I know why and I think you are also responsible for this change'.

'I am responsible?'

'Yes, you! How can you say that you know nothing about it?'

Anurupa's words put Seeta in a quandary. She remembers she has seen Hemanta at the meeting today. Can it be that it was not a whim, that he was there goaded by unprecedented thoughts and feelings and by the desire to find out real answers to his doubts? Maybe he was breaking through the cocoon of self-love. Indeed, she does not know for sure if he had actually left the meeting in boredom after a short time. Suppose he had not been able to pull himself away and had joined the rally to participate in the death-defying march!

Seeta is full of wonder. Hemanta had been particularly obstructive today in backing up his own position; but could that be because he has been trying to hide from Seeta the chinks in his armour? Was it necessary to defend his own obstinacy with such blind vehemence because he is in turmoil within, because his old beliefs are falling apart? Would Hemanta ever acknowledge to her that he had been mistaken? Does he have it in him? Seeta has no pleasure in winning this battle for herself; but she would be glad to know that Hemanta has the courage to acknowledge his mistake and would not be ashamed of accepting a new truth when he has perceived it.

Seeta makes Anurupa take a seat and rings up various people herself. After many efforts she is able to speak to Sibnath at the hospital. Sibnath has been looking after the injured.

He says, 'Who are you talking of? Hemanta? Yes, he is here'.

Seeta thinks to herself, 'Now we are in for it!'

'How is he?'

'Oh, it is just a scratch! Once the wound has been dressed he can get back home'.

'Was he at the rally?'

'He was'.

'And during the firing?'

'He was there throughout'.

'I find that surprising'.

'What is so surprising? Whose blood would not boil at what was happening?'

'He has never allowed his blood to boil except when arguing. Tell him to get back home as soon as he can. His mother is very worried'.

'No, no, please don't tell him anything about me, Seeta, they must not let him know about me', ejaculates Anurupa pleadingly.

'Sibnath, are you still there? Don't tell Hemanta anything about his mother. Just let him know that I called and asked him to go home'.

Let Hemanta know that Seeta is aware of what has happened and the morning's argument stands cancelled.

Anurupa continues to sit as if in a trance. Seeta can partly guess why her face has gone pale even after learning that her son is safe. The days of indecision and doubt are over for Hemanta. He cannot keep himself aloof from the world around him in his selfish interest any more. This is no more just a decision he has taken to himself; he has come out in rebellion. Anurupa looks defeated because her dreams of a happy future are about to founder.

'Auntie, what are you worrying about?'

'Why should I not worry? You may be bubbling with happiness over Hemanta putting his whole career in the backburner going to meetings, courting arrest and sacrificing all for his country; but have you considered me? Do you know how much hope I had put on Hemanta? God only knows how much ill you have brought me!'

Seeta says in surprise and pain, 'Auntie, how can you blame me for all this? What you are saying is childish. Your son has not changed because of his friendship with me; who am I to make such a tall claim? Hemanta's change is of his own choosing. When the country is in such turmoil, when politics is everywhere, don't you see that to save him from its influence you would have to lock him up at home? He may have to face heavier blows, can you prevent that? It is not me; even great leaders cannot awaken such change, we awaken on our own, who are leaders but intermediaries?'

A little later, she slowly adds, 'But is frustration all you feel? When a son suffers for his country and his people does not a mother feel proud of him too?'

Anurupa angrily says, 'What would you understand of it, Seeta? If you had to endure anything like what I have gone through to bring up my son properly, then you would have known how one feels to see that son giving up his studies and spoiling his future!'

'But, auntie, you are not being fair to Hemanta!'

'Indeed?'

'Why are you taking it for granted that he is going to give up his studies and spoil his future? If he is thinking about his country, does that exclude studies? Why should he court arrest out of nothing? By his courting arrest, the country cannot be saved. This is how Hemanta himself used to think, that if you are a student you should pursue your studies single-mindedly; or again if you join politics you give up everything else. Students must have a role in the fight for independence, but in the normal course that does not go against their studies; rather it gives them moral strength. How can you not see this, auntie?'

'May be because I am not clever like you!'

'You are angry now, later you may feel better about it'.

'Oh, I hope you do not think I shall let it go without a fight!'

Anurupa's vehemence and the bitterness showing on her distorted face surprises Seeta. Who does she want to hit out at in her helpless animosity? What is this fight she is talking of to make Hemanta turn away from the undesirable path? Is it going to be even more intense than her earlier fight to bring him up properly? But why should that make her look so hostile and resentful?

Seeta asks hesitantly, 'I do not understand you. With whom would you fight? About what?'

'Oh! I am not a child, Seeta, it has been fifteen years since I lost my husband's protection and have been running a household and bringing up my children on my own. You may think I am a fool, but I am not'.

Now it is clear to Seeta and she receives a severe jolt as she understands. She stares at Anurupa's face and it seems difficult now not to think of her as anything but entirely typical in the triviality of her suspicions.

'Auntie, never have I thought of you as a fool; but now I cannot help it. Are you thinking of fighting against me? Then you have really lost your senses. You may insult me if you like, but do you not see how you are insulting your own son when you say this? Do you think it is because of a girl and not because his own thoughts changed that he is going his own way and seeming to defy you? How could you think of your son as such a worthless creature when there is not a shred of truth in it? Do not stir up trouble without reason by making me the butt of your antagonism; it is only going to hurt you!'

Seeta says this with some ruthlessness because it seems to her that Anurupa is not likely to take her seriously unless she is quite open with her. She is actually appalled to see how far excess of mother's love can go, how it becomes an obsession turning into a curse of human life. And in this case, it plagues not a house-bound mother, who has nothing to do but to pour her unstinted love on her family, but one who has been on her own for the last fifteen years and has struggled to bring up her children against the heavy odds of the real world. This is what forces a child to give in to a mother's wishes and compromise; would Hemanta have to do the same? How would he find a way out of the problems his mother would otherwise create?

But maybe Anurupa would not make such trouble; after all she still has some hopes that Hemanta will complete his studies and get a good job. She is only suffering from unknown fears. Probably when she regains her calm, she might look at it from her son's point of view and admit that it is sheer folly to deny a grown-up son freedom of mobility and opinions and such vigilance on her part might defeat its very purpose. Seeta cannot quite believe that Anurupa will really wish to take matters to that unseemly level suggested by her words.

In fact, Anurupa has been sitting quite helplessly while Seeta rebukes her. Seeta cannot make out what her silence and immobility portends. She feels weary all over again and looks at Anurupa with doubtful eyes.

'I am somewhat taken aback by what you have just said, Seeta!'

Seeta is surprised when Anurupa utters these words in a timid manner and asks, 'But why should you be taken aback?'

After some hesitation Anurupa says in the same worried voice, 'You are not thinking of putting an end to your relationship with Hema because of what I told you just now? I do not want to be responsible for that!'

At any other time, this would have amused Seeta, but now it is the helplessness of the appeal that strikes her. Imagining her as Hemanta's future wife, Anurupa has gone beyond all bounds in the belief that the two of them are in love and have decided all such matters between themselves. There is not an inkling of doubt in her mind on this. Perhaps this is the reason why Anurupa was furious with her believing her to be the sole active cause behind Hemanta's betrayal.

It is the same old story of the tension-ridden relationship in the family between the mother and the daughter-in-law; only in this case the prospect of marriage is still distant. Seeta recalls old nursery rhymes and spells demonising the mother-in-law and thereby only proving the reality of what young daughters-in-law suffer. Even after death the former can only be saved from the tortures of hell by the daughter-in-law's ritual intervention. Anurupa is still alive and well; but is she already seeking redemption from the possible vengeance of her might-be daughter-in-law?

Seeta feels somewhat relieved however; Anurupa's attitude clearly tells her that for all her obsession she still has judgement enough to consider Hemanta's side of the question. However bitterly she might try to hold back Hemanta, if his happiness and peace is at stake, she will not continue to be obstinate and will seek to smooth out things. It would not come to the situation she had feared.

Or would it? How can Seeta believe that this mother, so completely absorbed in her son, would reshape her dreams about him just because he feels anxious or unhappy? Would she be in a mood to compromise when she remembers how she, a woman, has devoted herself to earning money to bring him up at such cost to herself? If once she gets hold of the notion that this is an act of betrayal by her son, would she have equanimity enough to look for some mutual understanding? Who knows? She can only hope for the best.

Anurupa's confused behaviour helps Seeta recover her own earlier sense of intimacy with her. She breaks into a smile and says firmly, 'Why, you are not yourself today, auntie, what rubbish are you thinking of? I think you should go home now. Let me send someone with you to reach you home'.

'Don't worry. I shall be able to get back myself'.

'You shouldn't even think of it. Let Nakul go with you'.

Seeta feels even more certain about Anurupa when she realises why the latter had been so anxious that Hemanta should not be informed that she was worrying after him. Anurupa is extremely apprehensive lest Hemanta should think that she is intruding upon his independence. She had been somewhat taken aback when Seeta told her that it was inappropriate for her to worry about her adult son just because he had not returned by early evening. Her fear was that Hemanta might be annoyed with her excess in having rushed out herself to look for him. He might think that he did not even have the freedom to come home late just once in his life.

YES, ANURUPA SUFFERS from all these fears and worries. But she is firm on one point. She cannot stand by silently when Hemanta is about to spoil his own life through an immature whim. To the best of her ability, she would oppose it and try to ward it off; if that annoys Hemanta there is nothing to be done about it.

She is waiting to confront him directly, only Seeta's warning has made her wary of entering the fray immediately upon his return. To get even with her adult son she must be careful to maintain her cool and keep her passions under control like Seeta. So, it takes time for the matter to come to a head. As long as Rama and Jayanta are about she speaks with Hemanta as on other days giving him no hint of what she thinks of his escapade. Hemanta narrates his experience of the day; Rama and Jayanta listen avidly. Anurupa utters not a word. Hemanta too observes his mother's changed mood, but waits for her to make the first move. Maybe, Ma is just gathering her own thoughts before coming out with it. No need to hurry her.

Dinner is over soon after Hemanta's return. Jayanta goes off to sleep. Rama too goes to bed after a short time. Then Anurupa takes her chance.

'Are you sleepy, Hema?'

'No, Ma. What is on your mind?'

'Do I have to say it?'

'Why not? Otherwise, how should I get to know it?'

'That is a new one. You do not understand what is on my mind? Then it is my misfortune'.

Hemanta is non-plussed. He realises from his mother's tone that he is not getting off easily today. All the weapons in her armoury, anger, displeasure, complaints, tears—are in readiness. If he allows his mother to have the first word, she will go for all of it. Hemanta concludes that he must be in command of this exchange.

Anurupa is about to say something, but he pre-empts her and says, 'Please listen to me for a moment. I know you have been shocked and disturbed. I am not going to argue with you. Nor shall

I disobey you. I am telling you straight that if there is something you do not wish me to do, I shall accept it. Now let me tell you what I have in mind and ask you for your opinion. Just tell me 'yes' or 'no', the matter will end there. We shall not bother about it again'.

Anurupa is baffled. This is not what she had in mind at all. She had not expected that Hemanta would refrain from arguing with her or even from persuading her to his side, but would rather leave the decision to her. Hemanta is ready to accept whatever decision she takes whether he likes it or not—this announcement floods her heart with joy; but also, the heavy burden of deciding for him loads her down with its gravity. As a mother she could have subjected her son even to her illogical whims and blown his arguments to the winds. But Hemanta has deliberately closed that option. He has elevated her as mother to the skies, but the possibility of crashing down to earth from that height has also been opened up.

Hemanta says calmly, 'You know everything that has happened. There will be a protest meeting tomorrow which I wish to attend. A rally may be taken out after that, I would like to join that too. It depends on what you tell me now'.

'But are you no more interested in your studies?'

'Why? What makes you think so?'

'If you get into such activities will your studies not suffer?'

'Is that all?' Hemanta smiles, 'I am not getting into such activities every day. All that this means is that I am protesting against an injustice. Can I call myself a human being if I do not even do such a small thing? How can I stop being a human being on the excuse that I am a student, Ma? We are not responsible for all these troubles after all!'

'But still the troubles are there. Today you escaped with a minor injury, but tomorrow you may even die!' Anurupa allows herself to utter this sentence, but Hemanta can see on her face the marks of deadly fear oppressing her body and mind as she says it.

Hemanta says softly, 'Yes, that is possible. I cannot give you any false assurance'.

'So?'

'Let me tell you, Ma,' says Hemanta in an almost suffocated voice, 'At last today I have found the answer to all such worries. Tell me, can you give up everything else just because you are a student? Suppose I find you or Rama being attacked by some hooligan; even if I know quite well that if I intervene my head may be crushed, I may have brain injury which shall put paid to my student life—can I stay away just because of that? Can my studies be my only consideration at that moment? Of course, this is a special situation. Even a student whose only aim in life is to complete his course has to forget about his studies in such a special situation. But surely that does not mean that in normal circumstances I would give up all thought of my studies.'

Anurupa sits in stony silence.

'Anyway,' Hemanta continues in a normal tone 'I have told you I am not going to argue with you on this. Just tell me, is it 'yes' or 'no'?'

As if wounded to the quick, Anurupa cries out in anguish, 'How can I say 'yes' when I know you could die?'

'Indeed, it is difficult for you. Then you can do something else. Don't say anything. Leave it to me and trust my discretion. Yes, that is what you can do.'

Anurupa heaves a sigh. 'I should have known it, Hema. There is no stopping you.'

In this way mother and son reach a compromise which still keeps alive the tension between them. A mother's permission carries her blessing with it. This remained unachieved by Hemanta. But even the fact that he is able to avoid a mother's denial which signifies a curse indicates without doubt a change in the affection-ridden heart of a well-bred mother like Anurupa. Is it possible to say that soon she might be able to bless her son and say, alright, if you are going to your death how can I as a mother imagine a more honourable one for you?

OH RASUL, YOUR arm—are you going to lose it altogether?' Amina's wail of anguish tears apart the freezing midnight.

Rasul replies stubbornly, 'I still have the other'.

'True'. Amina restrains herself and stops her wail midway. What mother can show self-restraint when her son appears at midnight with blood-stained clothes and with his useless arm dangling from a sling around his neck? But Amina has felt her strength of mind increasing all the time ever since she has come to realise that her son is ready to die for the independence of his country and might face death any day.

'But why aren't you cuddling me, Ma? I have come to you to be cuddled!'

'It is such trouble being your Ma, Rasul, that I would rather not cuddle you' says Amina pressing Rasul's head fervently to her breast, 'I felt relieved when I heard you had been taken to the hospital. Don't I know that you are going to leave me one day, if not today then tomorrow or the day after. If it is over sooner rather than later at least you don't have to feel sorry about me all the time, nor do I have to worry about you constantly . . .'.

'Shall I tell you something, Ma?' says Rasul in a whisper.

'What?' Amina's voice is lowered too.

'They had kept me back at the hospital, but I was missing you so much that I quietly escaped'.

'What! The doctor instructed you to rest and you escaped and came here on foot walking more than a mile?'

'How could I endure such pain without a caress from you?'

Rasul feels his mother weeping silently. He has lost so much blood that his body is flagging with weakness and his feelings too are blurred and exhausted. Rasul knows that the fathomless melancholy overwhelming him to find Amina weeping is temporary and a reaction of losing blood to this extent. Otherwise, it is not like him to come at midnight just to provoke his mother's tears; even if he came, it was more his nature to make her forget her woes with exuberant gaiety. But today his mind has turned so soft that he is even finding some enjoyment in the pain of watching his mother break down. Indeed, the doctor had said that when you lose blood it affects your mind in strange ways and that therefore he should not suddenly try to leave the bed on his own imagining himself to be strong enough. That is just what he has done. He has left his bed and walked a whole mile to get home to see his mother in tears.

Rasul clenches his teeth and reminds himself, no, it is not because of his demented state that he is here to watch his mother cry. It was a thoughtful decision and he will not allow it to be diluted by his weakness. It was not just because he has been feeling weak but because he was arrested while in hospital that he felt so strongly that he must see his mother without delay. Nobody knows when they are going to meet again, so it is important that he should calm down his mother and allay her fears; that is his purpose in coming here, not to gratify himself with the sight of his mother crying for him.

'Well, if you are going to cry, I had better go'.

'Am I crying?'

'You may start howling if I tell you something else that I have to say!'

'Indeed!'

'I am not joking. There is more trouble to come and that is why I am here to see you in the middle of the night'.

So, Amina needs to brace herself anew brushing back her tears. If now her son is expecting more dangers then she has to give him courage, not burden him with her own fears. Rasul too had been pretty sure that it would be easier for Amina to get a hold on herself if she knew him to be in trouble. It was not enough that Rasul's arm had been shattered by a bullet, further peril awaited him—this knowledge would make his mother postpone her tears.

'I am under arrest'.

'Under arrest? What for?'

'Because I was present at the trouble spot.'

'It is you who have been hit by a bullet and you are to be arrested!'

'That is evidence that I have been present there; otherwise, how did I get hit?'

'Wonderful!'

Rasul has no more to say, he really feels worn out. It is not that he feels regret, but that calm solemn mood of depression still possesses him.

Amina gently runs her fingers through his hair. Many questions crowd her mind. A few of them can be articulated. The rest will remain to haunt her.

'Were you arrested and then sent to the hospital?'

'No, I was arrested in the hospital itself'.

'Could you get bail?'

'No, there is no provision of bail'.

'Then?'

'I eluded them so that I could come and meet you. Must return before morning'.

'Why do you have to return?'

'What else can I do? Some others have also been arrested; they are all there. If I do not go back people will say that your son was one of the arrested, but he got away on his own'.

'Alright, go to sleep now; no more words'.

What Amina perceives to some extent is that injury and loss of blood caused some kind of reaction which filled Rasul with this irresistible urge to come and see her. He had tried to fight against it, but had ultimately given in. Does he have some hidden regret in his mind about not being like other peace-abiding studious youth, about bringing more sorrow to his unhappy mother through the dangerous path he has been following in his precipitate eagerness for his country's freedom? But she has never given him cause to think that she rues it. Also are there so many peace-loving studious young men to be found today that Rasul can contrast himself with them and feel guilty for loving his country to the extent of distressing his mother? Amina feels they are all like her Rasul—they have no other way. Rasul sleeps on heavily; occasional moans of pain escape his lips. Amina sits wide awake close by looking at his pallid features.

The night is almost over when Abdul enters.

'We must leave now, Rasul'.

'Does he have to walk all the way?' asks Amina.

'No. We managed to get a vehicle'.

Abdul too has spent a sleepless night; his eyes are blood-shot. As she stares at those eyes the deep silence of the last hours of the city night seems to pose this question to her: Is it just one son you have?

It is the son of her womb who has made distinctions redundant for her. It seems she is nursing countless unknown injured sons at her breast together with Rasul. It has so happened that he has brought with him a friend whom she has known only for a short time, but who seems to be as close as Rasul, nurtured with her heart's blood.

AS ON OTHER occasions, it is Sudha who opens the front door for him. She does not look into his eyes today with silent reproach, but moves aside to let him pass with bowed head.

Akshay asks cheerfully, 'Has everyone gone to sleep?'

'I don't know. Please don't shout'.

'What is the matter with you?'

Sudha does not respond. With bowed head she waits for Akshay to get in and proceeds inside without a word after closing the front door. Akshay watches with mixed feeling. Today for the first time he can actually see how keenly Sudha has suffered for his drunkenness; of course, her suffering must be keener today because she thinks not only has Akshay got drunk, but he has done so breaking his solemn vow not to get drunk. Is it not a natural reaction for one who has seen him go deeper into his addiction every day, enduring the torture of not knowing where this would end? Since he had never thought of this earlier, Akshay's sympathy for her had been a matter of whim, coming like a light cloud and evaporating at will. Since for the first time tonight after a long while he has not returned in a besotted state like an insensate beast, he can see clearly how brutally he has tormented Sudha. He burns with the first feelings of genuine remorse. But then he also realizes that tonight he is drunk with the sense of his own abstinence. Tomorrow he is likely to torment Sudha again if only he takes enough booze to compensate for today. Sudha is all the more terrified today because of the manner in which he had raised hell only last night. As soon as he had reached home, he had accosted her with: 'You old witch with your loose dugs, what do you think of yourself, eh? A bashful bride dressed up in all that sari and chemise? Take them off, I say, take them off at once!'

How can Sudha forget? She is waiting for another bout of violent drunkenness; only she does not know what form it will take.

He has to do much penance, he thinks, a long process of tearing and crushing and crumbling up his own self. He not only has to bear up with the hideous, uncontrollable lust for getting drunk, but also with the oppressive mistrust of his family and acquaintances about his having really done away with his addiction. It is a hard task to uphold this moment of rebellion when he has refused to drink even when he had the chance and has resolved to give up his addiction. It is another terrifying addiction that has kept him absorbed, addiction to the desire to face police bullets and die so that he and others may live. This new addiction has made him so clear-headed that he perceives that he may yield to his weakness for the bottle once or twice, but from now on he would be repelled even while lifting his drink to his mouth by the thought that what he is drinking is the fresh bubbling blood of living young people.

Such bizarre thoughts pass through Akshay's head. Only tonight he is totally enthralled with the thought of a grand release, reality at the end of a nightmare. His heart swells up when he thinks how he can bring back the light of joy and hope to Sudha's death-pale features. It recalls to him the surging pleasure of discovering one's first love for the first time. As he changes his outdoor clothes he cannot turn his eyes away from Sudha. She is sitting on the cot, eyes fixed to the ground. She might have laid herself down, face turned towards the wall; but Akshay knows why she is unable to do that. It has been her responsibility always to bear the brunt of Akshay's drunkenness and to see that he does not, at the dead of night, start a ruckus that would bring shame to the family. She never lies down until Akshay does; she never sleeps until Akshay does. She has been mortified by Akshay's behaviour today, but she must still do her duty. Akshay feels a thousand springs blooming in his heart. To please his wife of some years he will not just inform her of his abstinence, but will make this desolate humiliated woman blossom out in joy again by confessing his love for her. It shall be a new wedding-day for them once more.

'Has Ma gone to sleep, Sudha?'[19]

'How should I know?'

'Let me go and see'.

Sudha stifles her wail of fear and asks, 'Why?'

'I want to touch her feet', with this Akshay leaves the bedroom and turns the corner of the verandah to reach his mother's room. Akshay's sister Lalita shares it with her. But Akshay has to stop midway even as he turns the corner, because Sudha has prostrated herself at his feet.

'I beg of you, do not create trouble at this time of night; Ma must be sleeping'.

Akshay says in surprise: 'What is this? Why are you stopping

[19] A typical middle-class family in the urban milieu would consist of, apart from the man who is the main bread-earner and his wife, children, if any, and dependent parents and siblings. This is how Akshay's mother and sister form part of the household. Sudha has the unenviable task of keeping Akshay's drunken behaviour hidden for the sake of respectability not only from neighbours, but also from his mother.

me? Don't you see why I wish to touch Ma's feet at this time of night? I did not drink today. She will be happy to know'.

'She feels unwell if her sleep is disturbed. Tell her in the morning'.

Akshay feels discouraged to think that Sudha does not believe his words.

'I am telling you the truth, Sudha. I did not drink today'.

'I know. But please do not disturb Ma. Come to the bedroom'.

'Alright, I have to convince you first'.

Following him to the room, Sudha says, 'Why don't we go to sleep? I am feeling sleepy too; let us go to bed now'.

'But what about my dinner?'

'Have you had no dinner? But on other days. . . . Then please come and eat'.

Sudha spreads out a hand-made cloth mat on the floor for him to sit on. His well-covered food was waiting for him in a corner of the bedroom, the hand-made mat had been kept neatly tucked up on the clothes-stand. Akshay hardly ever has dinner at home, but every evening it is kept in readiness for him, whether he eats it or not.

Akshay slowly takes his seat. He still sits without touching his food even after everything has been properly laid out in front of him. He even forgets to blink watching Sudha in her housewifely mission. Tonight, he has not taken a whiff of alcohol, yet Sudha believes him to be drunk. But even so, she has not given up her faith and her hope. That means she is not dead as he had thought; she is a living person. His betrayal of his promise had shocked her, but she is already trying to overcome that shock and to persuade herself that—not today or tomorrow-- but maybe one day he is going to succeed; she is trying to come to terms with life in the indomitable urge to live.

To die means nothing. So, he had thought that Sudha would end her life if he came back drunk today. What he had not known is the extent of concern Sudha has for staying alive, so that even if dying might have been easier she has chosen to struggle to live refusing to take the latest example of his failure as ultimate. Akshay had always thought of Sudha as an ordinary wife to whom her husband was all-in-all. It is not that she is an extraordinary person. But for the first time in his life, he feels overwhelmed trying to gauge the depth of the fighting spirit of an ordinary woman in her struggle for existence.

'You do not believe me?'

'But of course. Now eat'.

'I am telling you the truth. I shall hide nothing from you, Sudha; the credit is not mine. It would be false to say that my promise not to drink held me up. I had almost reached the hotel and might have even boozed more than usual. But it was what I saw today, Sudha, what struck me dumb was the unbelievable courage of those I used to think of as raw romantic excitable youth. It made me feel that all my thinking was wholly mistaken. I was on the threshold of the hotel to have my booze thinking all the while what sort of addiction it might be that could make an ordinary youth go and face bullets knowing he may be killed. Without being drunk what addiction could lead them to do so and why do I then spend good money like a fool for this cheap unpleasant addiction of mine? It was those boys who prevented me from getting drunk. It has nothing to do with my own strength of mind'.

'Oh, alright', says Sudha in a weary tone of dejection, 'I shall hear all about it tomorrow'.

Akshay is flabbergasted. Sudha is still not prepared to believe him and thinks he is talking meaninglessly. She merely thinks that he is more sozzled than usual and has graduated from making a ruckus to waxing philosophical.

'But you could have smelt it from my breath if I had drunk'.

'Don't worry about that. Who is to smell your breath? You can gurgle and brush your teeth in the morning'.

'Look, can you smell me?' He takes his mouth close to Sudha's. He should have done it earlier to convince Sudha. His mind is steeped in perverted sentiments. That is why he has been indulging in all this tall talk so late at night, such as would make even a person unfamiliar with his habits suspect drunkenness.

'It is true; you have not been drinking!'

'Indeed, I am telling you the truth'.

Sudha's face changes now. At last, she is convinced, and still not quite able to believe her own good fortune.

'Well, does it mean much—abstaining for once?'

'You are right'. Akshay agrees without taking offence. Sudha can tolerate his breaking promise for once in the hope that this is not the end and some day, he will be able to keep his word. This is what Akshay learnt a short while back. Now he hardly feels hurt by Sudha's hint that a day's abstinence is nothing out of the common and only when he is able to abstain tomorrow, the day after and the next day may his freedom from addiction be proved. What she has said is true. Tonight, of all nights Akshay refuses to be foolishly offended by the truth.

The urge to go and touch his mother's feet evaporates. His mind had been so highly strung that he had lost his sense of reality. Sudha has brought him back to his senses; the eccentric action of disturbing his mother at dead of night just to touch her feet would of course be interpreted as a drunkard's whim.

He feels relieved that he can understand simple matters without resorting to needless complications. Of course, the underlying addictive urge, the intolerable sense of an ending, of the blind terror that there is no chance tonight of getting a drop to drink even if he beats his head against the wall still persists.

THE DEEP BLUE neon sign indicating 'Electricals Limited' can be seen from a distance. As far as the eye goes straight ahead from the turning stretches the smooth broad arterial road, with magnificent buildings on either side. Signs of the developing metropolis! The narrow sleazy lanes and slums are invisible behind these great edifices planned before the War and begun as proof of the growing numbers of the affluent in this city. Everything had been postponed since the outbreak of the War and mammoth skeleton structures of steel here and there still bore testimony to how suddenly all such initiatives had stopped. During nights of black-out even these roads had been in darkness. Now that the War is over, numerous electric lights are lit once more to give the impression of full-moon night even on darkest evenings.

'Electricals Limited' is one of the five big emporia on the ground floor of a three-storied building. This is a legitimate business owned by N. Dasgupta. Since the War he has also been running many under-the-counter enterprises; as everybody knows the War may be over, but such illicit dealings are still being carried on with a flourish as long as they may last. He himself lives in a flat on the first floor to the north of the building; but the flat just above it has also been kept on rent by him under a false name. He operates it as unlicensed hotel, bar and night-club offering service to various people. High-ups visit the place with female companions in the evening, sometimes staying overnight. Many high-up people who do not know where to take their female companions at midnight contact other high-ups whose nod allows them to seek this flat as a safe nook. Dinner, snacks, drinks and beds—everything is provided here without stint.

Dasgupta puts down the receiver and keeps on staring blankly in front of him for a long time. In this sort of business troubles arise unexpectedly from wholly inconsequential matters. Big deals amounting to many thousands are clinched smoothly; one does not have to worry for a single moment where major risks are involved. It is in matters involving a few hundred rupees that such hitches occur. On quite a few earlier occasions, Ganesh had transported goods to the same address. Dasgupta would not have thought in his dreams that he would be caught in trouble on the way and create trouble for Dasgupta himself.

Even the thought enrages him. Is it not sheer bad luck that

danger should strike from the least anticipated quarter? He feels even more furious to think that the stupid bumpkin must have stopped on the road out of curiosity at the hullabaloo going on around him and died of a bullet meant for those degenerate boys out on a rampage making a show of heroism for their perverse ends. If Ganesh's name and identity were discovered it would surely come out that Dasgupta had hired him to transport contraband goods. Who would look after his interests at the hospital? Who would realise that the matter has to be hushed up? A lot of pother can be expected. His name would inevitably be dragged into it. The same big bosses whose itching palms he does his best to keep oiled with money would be forced to sacrifice him to save their own skin.

Perhaps he will be able to save the situation without much damage done. But his prestige would surely suffer if it became public that contraband foreign liquor gets transported from his emporium of electrical goods in cases for radio sets. Can something be done about it? He has so many acquaintances in influential circles; cannot the matter be hushed up before it breaks out?

Dasgupta calls, 'Chander!'

'Chander is in the flat upstairs, Babu!'

''Call him! Right now!'

The wily Chander, Dasgupta's most trusted factotum, appears. He is middle-aged, corpulent, with a round face. He had a little bit of college education which helped to sharpen his wits. He is more-or-less in charge of the apartment upstairs, keeping rich and middling clients happy and fattening himself on the leavings. He keeps accounts, rules over other servants with an iron hand, provides high society women in search of prey with their needs maintaining due discretion through his inexorable commands. Where necessary, he rarely shies away from boot-licking and even helps worthy patrons with his own hands to uncork their soda water bottles.

Even before Dasgupta can utter a word, he asks in a casual

voice, 'So Ganesh is not back, Babu? What can have happened? He has only to hand over the goods, no money passes his hands. It is not as if he could have felt tempted by money and ran off. He is not such a smart guy that he would run off with the goods!'

Dasgupta ponders over the question as to whether he should confide in Chander. The latter is his mainstay, expert at judging people and is the one who had suggested that Ganesh's movements should be confined to the emporium on the ground floor; he must have no inkling of what happened on the second-floor flat. He himself had not paid much attention to all this. On his own he would have thought that a chuckle-headed village boy like Ganesh would be more suitable as a servant upstairs. In fact, Ganesh had been sent once or twice on small errands for the clients at the apartment. From what Cameron had said over the phone it was evident that Ganesh's death had taken place before he could inform anyone about himself. Otherwise, why should they call up Cameron from the hospital? Suppose if Ganesh had lived to give a statement when he reached the hospital, then the whole story of the second-floor apartment might have come out! Dasgupta gets the jitters even as he contemplates that.

'Some news about Ganesh has come, Chander. There is a hitch. How many people are there upstairs today?'

'Many are absent because of the troubles in the city. Dutta Sahib is there, Binoybabu is there, Peter Sahib, Roybabu, Ghosh Sahib....

'Ghosh Sahib is there?'

'He is. He has come with a very young girl today, hardly more than fifteen. She started throwing up just after having a sip. . . .' Chandra announces with a strange lop-sided snigger. 'But what about Ganesh, Babu?'

'Oh, like the silly ass he was, he got caught in the troubles. He died hit by a stray bullet. They have taken the dead body to the hospital together with the package. They rang up Cameron about his identity. He has been to Cameron's twice. Why did he have to be given a slip of paper with Cameron's name and address on it? That Sudhir is a damned fool!'

Chandra listens and absorbs all the information without batting an eyelid.

'Have you decided what is to be done, Babu?'

'I am thinking of telling Ghosh. If he tries, he can easily take charge of the package and settle things'.

Chander demurs.

'He can if he tries. But he is still taking advantage of that earlier occasion. He hardly had to do anything, yet he is cashing on it. He is even reluctant to pay for his drinks. If you ask him for a favour again, he will have us at an advantage'.

Dasgupta nods and agrees. He ejaculates with irritation, 'What can be done? These people are so powerful; to do business you have to keep on their right side. Ghosh is the most shameless of the whole bunch. Others help with the business and take money for it; but they make payments for the services here. Ghosh is quite brazen. It is true that the bastard will have us at an advantage; but you see the case has to be removed before they open it. I would not have worried otherwise. But that boy was killed by a bullet; that is what makes the situation sticky'.

Chander still feels unhappy. It is not just that Ghosh Sahib wants to enjoy all the pleasures and comforts of the flat upstairs without paying for them; he also tries to deprive Chander himself of his dues. He merely pays him small tips, as if he is an ordinary hotel-boy. Actually, Ghosh Sahib behaves as if the flat is his own and treats the servants as if they owe their wages to him.

'There could be a way out'.

'Why don't you tell me? Show us how clever you are'.

'You could yourself go and identify Ganesh and have the case restored to you. Once you have got it, who is to know what is inside! Whatever you say will go'.

Dasgupta marvels at this display of quick wit on Chander's part. He also feels riddled with envy. Since cunning is his own principal asset which he has to use all the time and since he prides himself for the heady success he has acquired through this, he finds its presence in others a real surprise.

'I have thought about it, Chander, but it is a case of manslaughter and there is no stamp on the case to identify the owner. Suppose they do not release it? If there is an accredited government officer to identify it then that might be safer'.

'Take a letter from Peter Sahib'.

'If I tell him he will demand a thousand'.

'You don't have to tell him. You don't need a letter as the proprietor of the goods. He just has to write a two-line general credential saying he knows you. Tell him you are asking him for it just in case there is some need. He will gladly do it if you give him a bottle of Scotch'.

This evidence of Chander's cleverness fascinates Dasgupta all the more even while his heart burns with jealousy. This is in spite of the fact that he knows Chander serves him, even calls him 'babu'. For a few moments, it seems to him that it is Chander who is running the whole business just putting him up as a front. Chander is far more intelligent than him. True, the major share of the earnings comes to him, but even that is Chander's strategy. He may be earning more, but Chander is playing safe while all the responsibility, all the risks lie on his shoulders. Chander's takings are not meagre either. If one calculates from Chander's starting-point relative to his own at the outbreak of the War, would not one come to the conclusion that Chander has been hundred times more a gainer than him? Chander would hardly have been able to run a business on such grand scale without the support of someone like himself. To become so big, he needed someone who had at least a nodding acquaintance with educated affluent upper-class people with a certain life style. He has more property, more influence, more of responsibility; so why should Chander grudge him a greater share of the takings? His dreams are unfulfilled. He has acquired much; but has had to pay for it too. Chander is bleeding him white; if he makes ten thousand Chander's share should be no more than ten; but he is pinching a thousand instead of that while he, Dasgupta, has no other way but to bear it because he cannot do without Chander, who seems to be the one running the show.

Dasgupta has felt this heartburn on earlier occasions too, but never so keenly. As the pride of achievement sinks like a deflated balloon, he feels the agony of a suicide for a few moments.

But soon he recovers himself completely. Cheap people get inflated just with a little puff of air. What are Chander's assets? Say, twenty or even twenty-five thousand? And he is feeling so agitated because of that! It is as if a king should envy the pickings of his lesser officials!

'Babu . . .

'Wait, wait' says Dasgupta like an army chief outlining a plan, 'I have taken stock of all that. Your words have reminded me of something else. Unless it is absolutely necessary, I do not wish to go and identify Ganesh. I recall now that a lot of chaos is going on at the hospital; there may be some opportunity of abstracting the case quietly. Peter's letter may be used only if there is some row. We can always say it contains something perishable like fruits which would go bad if not removed immediately. Then we can go and identify Ganesh; but I do not think there will be any problem. Who would want to make a fuss over the body of a mere shop-attendant?'

Chander humbly says, 'How sharp you are, Babu!'

OSMAN WAKES UP from sleep in his little room in a slum near Sealdah. Many people are up already, they are speaking in many voices. It comes to Osman as a mixed noise and to his waking consciousness, immediately takes the shape of those words uttered by Ganesh: 'Are they not going to move?' It is as if his dreams have been re-sounding with them; he wakes up to the words rather than hears them after waking up.

In his empty room as the words come to him like echoes of his own mind they get mixed up with his thoughts of his wife and children back home.

He is not going to the factory today. No one should, neither he nor anybody else. Osman feels charged with immense confidence and determination. If people were able to get together in their resolve to go ahead without waiting for leaders to give the green signal, then they would surely unite without being told to against the senseless brutality unleashed on them. He not only endorses that decision from the depths of his own mind, but he feels it being confirmed by the noises outside. At first it is not clear to him. Then as he comes out of his room the sound of many voices tells him that those who pour out of the slum every day even before morning to join work are all there. If they had intended to go to work, they would not have stayed on to congregate in the space outside their rooms and engage in excited talk in the light of dawn. Usually if he is late in getting up, either Rahman or Siddique, Golam or someone else gives him a call on the way out. He now understands why no one has done so today. They have decided not to go to the factory; they have assumed without asking him that he would do the same. So why call up a sleeping man needlessly?

At his own factory, the process of building a union is getting hampered again and again due to devilish manoeuvres. He has been suffering from regret ever since he resigned from his job in the tramways and joined this place. He always feels a deep urge to be part of a large union where all workers would come together. But in this factory somehow, he has been missing that opportunity.

On the other hand, on that last occasion the tram workers' union had given ample proof of their unity.[20] Since that time he has

[20] The Calcutta Tram Workers' Union, founded in 1928–29, was one of the best-organized and most militant unions where communists had undoubted leadership. Between December 1945 and January 1946 many trade unions took up militant struggles and strike actions in Bengal. The Tram Workers' Union was among them. Osman may be referring to this.

been feeling even more lonesome. He has constantly thought how he might have been one of them and prided himself on having a place among thousands of people who had linked arms to fight. He had felt this emptiness till yesterday and then everything had been thrown apart by an upheaval. Waking up today he not only finds himself relieved of the sense of being left out, but he has got more than he had hoped for. Inside his room he had decided on his own not to go to work; but now in the company of others he finds that it is not he alone, but all of them have taken the same resolve. If that is so, who can tell how many countless thousands of minds, even if unknown to him, have linked arms with him on this?

Khalil says, 'Dada,[21] what a business! All public transport is closed, tramcars, buses, the whole works . . .'.

Osman says, 'No wonder! This is only expected'.

Rezzak gets excited and says, 'Why don't we stop the trains too? If we go and lie down on the line, they will all come to a standstill and go on blowing their whistles!'

Osman says, 'Indeed no! Stopping trains would not be right'.

Many people have gathered at the mucky open space near the community tube well next to the long red-bricked wall. Old nani, grandma to everybody, bent down with age and hobbling with slow steps to the tube well to pour a little water over her body and take back some in her tin container for later use also stops for a while on the way. Women ask questions in an agitated manner, want to get more details and make angry comments on the happenings. The pressure of indignation and outrage transform the faces of men and women putting the stamp of patience and urgency on them. Each word, each pause, each intake of breath, each look signifies protest. Centuries of inhumanity and centuries of outrage seem to have erupted in protest over yesterday's events. It is no wonder that even while shivering under their meagre clothings on

[21] 'Dada' literally means 'elder brother' and has been used in this sense more than once in the novel. Here the term is an acknowledgement of Osman's relative seniority and the fact that he is respected in the bustee.

this cool winter morning, many of them should find their teeth on edge because of the boiling heat within.

Then Hanif strolls into their midst.

His words are provocative and deadly. He seems to want to arouse the agitated people to frenzy and works himself up to frenzy in the process.

'Come let us all go. There are going to be big troubles today. Why should we stay back? There will be lots of people with us. Let us go and smash up all the shops. We just have to start, see what ruckus breaks out . . .'

Budhulal is standing behind him; he says, 'Cheers! Cheers!'

Some of the younger boys grow restive, but the others seem to have become even calmer. Those who had been gnashing their teeth slowly slacken their jaws.

'What are you saying, mian? Have you gone mad?' Osman says.

Hanif snarls, 'Mad? Am I?'

'We shall go and smash up shops and then goondas will come and loot them. Is that what we want?' Osman raises his voice so that everyone can hear him, 'What is all this talk of smashing up shops? Have a meeting, have a rally, put your tools down in protest. Let shops remain closed. That is all.'

'And may I know who you are calling a goonda?' Hanif moves towards him in a threatening manner. Some of the others press close to him to stop Hanif if he should go beyond limits.

'Who should I call a goonda? Aren't there many such around? If we attack shops it will be mayhem for them, who doesn't know that?'

'You are growing too big for your shoes,' Hanif threatens.

'Don't you try to create trouble, Hanif!' Siddiq intervenes, advancing one step towards Hanif. Some others move closer to Osman.

After a moment of hesitation, Hanif leaves with his companions. Budhulal turns around a couple of times on his way to stare at Osman, meaning, alright, maybe another time! Budhulal is a notorious leader of armed gangs in this area. He has even more clout than Hanif.[22]

IN ANOTHER HALF-HOUR Osman is out on the road. He will go to the hospital a little later to find out about Ganesh, no use reaching there early. On his way, he is keen to visit Rasul's place. He feels impatient to meet him and talk to him once more. He had always felt drawn to Rasul seeing in him similarities with his own son in courage, in intelligence, even in his foolhardy mistakes, but never has he felt the pull as strongly as today.

His mind is in turmoil in so many ways today; in the midst of all that the shadowy contours of a future possibility relating to his family appear. His daughter Paribanu is of marriageable age and in every letter from home her mother keeps on reminding Osman that he should think seriously of finding a groom for her. Proposals are coming from within his circle of relatives, but not a single one has come up to the standards he has in his mind about the future groom for his daughter. He had been looking for the son he has lost in his prospective son-in-law. Not that he is wholly conscious of this strange fancy he nurtures in his mind. Had he been aware, he would have been more wary about it. But he does not even know how he has been working out in the depths of his own mind glimpses of the possibility of giving Paribanu in marriage to Rasul.

[22] Hanif the Muslim gangster takes the main role here because the slum in the narrative is dominated by Muslim workers. This is why Budhulal, although he is said to be an even bigger gangster, remains in the background. In the rising incidents of communal violence in and around Calcutta from the 1930s, these gangsters would be willing tools of motivated political elements as trained perpetrators of murder and mayhem. During the notorious 'Great Calcutta Killings' of August 16, 1946, it was the Budhulals and Hanifs, secure in their political patronage, who took over Calcutta for a few days. This episode in the novel, however, is meant to recall other real-life occasions when their machinations did not work because the ordinary residents of the slum prevented them.

Rasul lives not very far. But it takes Osman a long time to get there. Already people are gathering on the road and there is a soft united hum of protest rising from them. Osman has seen larger gatherings at public festivals, but the tumult today is quite different from festive hubbub. Here the joint tone gives vent to one emotion, anger. There are hardly any vehicles on the road. One private car is stopped right in front of Osman and made to go back. The next moment, another car is also stopped, but after a few words to the man inside, the crowd moves apart to let it pass and two young men escort it right up to the corner beyond the crowds.

'It is a doctor's car', someone responds to Osman's query.

Is this happening in other parts of the city too? Osman thinks. Vehicles carrying armed police pass by, provoking cries of Jai Hind! Inquilab Zindabad! Down with imperialism! What is going to happen if the powers that be again engage in the tomfoolery of trying to stop this expression of sorrow and anger with batons and bullets is the thought uppermost in Osman's mind.

Amina opens the front door herself. Her eyes marked with sleeplessness alarm Osman and he bursts out, 'Rasul . . . ?'

'He went back to the hospital. Do come in and sit down'.

She gives Osman a seat made of woven cane to sit on and seats herself on the stool Rasul uses with his study table of cheap timber. The cover of the cane seat is a work of beauty; it is made of cloth and embroidered with coloured threads taken out of old sari borders.

'Why did he go back?'

Amina's account and explanation of Rasul's home-coming and subsequent return to the hospital strikes Osman silent for several minutes.

'A lot of blood he has lost!'

'That is the worry now', says Amina haltingly.

Osman says, 'I have heard they preserve blood in bottles and give transfusions to patients'.

'That is what they would have done to him, but it seems he is refusing it because blood is in short supply and there are others who need it more'.

'That is true'.

All of a sudden, the desire to make Rasul his son-in-law takes clear shape and bursts like a strong tidal wave on Osman's mind. 'Let me go to the hospital and see him'.

In spite of knowing that this is just not the right moment for such proposals—who knows how Amina will take it—Osman can no longer check his heart's bidding and begins, 'I have a request; let me put it to you right now. You have seen my daughter, Paribanu; she is grown up now'.

'But of course. I have seen her quite a few times'.

Amina feels surprised at this sudden reference to Paribanu.

'I am looking for a groom for her. My request to you is that after Rasul comes back, you will have to accept my daughter. I am a worker, a truck driver. My daughter will not disappoint you.'

'It is a welcome proposal', says Amina sincerely, 'Only thing is that Rasul has to give consent'.

'That goes without saying. Rasul's consent must come first'.

Amina keeps her sharp yearning in check and asks casually, 'Can I come with you?'

'You wish to come?' Osman sounds worried, 'You will have to walk all the way. Troubles may break out at any time. It is better to go later. Let me visit him now. On my way back home, I shall let you know how he is faring'.

'Then that is better'.

Amina knows the history of Osman's loss of his son, a young energetic lad like her own Rasul, but at loggerheads with him about the path to be followed for the country's freedom. Full of spirit, he made no bones about his convictions. Amina had learnt from Osman that he had been in two minds for the first time about the last order he got from Khan Sahib. Later three days before dying in hospital he had admitted his mistake to his father and had said, 'Khan Sahib left us to face the music escaping in the Sub-divisional

Officer's car; my leg got crushed under its back wheel, but that is not what I blame him for. How should I know that he had sent us to beat up the tenants? Today he came to the hospital and told me that I must name such and such tenants for having attacked us. So the cat came out of the bag. Those tenants had been at a peasants' meeting in another area. How could they have attacked us? You were right. Let me get back this time. I shall never jump into a fray again without going into its depth. I shall pay heed to you and to Ziauddin Sahib'. These words, this language, uttered just three days before he died, had been repeated exactly by Osman after he had lost his son and perhaps because of that they have been emblazoned on her mind like the oft-repeated words of a manifesto. Osman had expected his son to live, not to die within three days. Even as she thinks about it tears of deep sympathy for him well out of Amina's eyes.

They are still talking and Osman is just about to bid her goodbye when Seeta comes with news of Rasul. On the way, she has been trying to work out just how to break the news about her hospitalised son to a mother, to what extent to balance her justified fears with hopes. Rasul is on the mend; he will recover within a few days. This is the main news she has to convey. But there is a small thing causing worry and that is not to be entirely brushed aside. Amina should be informed of that too. It would be an act of cruelty to tell her today that she has nothing to fear and then to have to break the worst news tomorrow.

She had thought of all the things she was going to say on her way, but now she dispenses with her pre-arranged speech and decides it would be better to put it simply and openly.

'I am coming from Rasul. He is better and is sleeping now'.

'But then why. . . ?'

'Do not be anxious. He had lost a lot of blood and the exertion of coming home and then getting back has made him weaker. He is being given blood and is going to recover quickly. His extreme weakness of course is a bit of a worry.'

Both the listeners heave such a sigh of relief together that Seeta is startled; then they say, 'That is a bit of a worry of course.'

Feeling a little relieved by their response Seeta carries on: 'That is just what I was saying. The blood will help him to get better; there only remains the possibility of after-shock. But that may happen any way in surgical cases, even in cases of childbirth. . . .'

Seeta looks at Amina and stops embarrassed.

Amina says in a normal voice, 'You are quite right. This bit of trouble I am carrying now after a gap of nine years will have to be delivered in another two or three months; who knows I may even die in giving birth. My man has been in jail for the last two months; I have got three letters from him till now. All his worry is about what is happening to me. Yes, dear, he is more worried about me than about his eldest son. He knows what his son's views are and is convinced that he will carry on in his own way unless someone murders him. What is more, he thinks his son is an adult person now and if he dies like a man . . .'.

Seeta has heard of Rasul's mother from various people, but had not expected her even then to respond in this way. Apart from Rasul, she only has another ten-year-old son for support as she is coping with the situation in this state. Does it even cross her mind what she is going to do with Rasul in jail? This question must surely have troubled her; but she seems to be confident of being able to cope. She is not someone to give up and leave everything in the hands of fate.

Out of the blue Seeta asks her, 'Did you observe purdah at any time?'

Amina says emphatically, 'Didn't I? What do you think? Bengali women have not got rid of their purdah even today. Why speak in the past tense?'[23]

[23] Seeta's question obviously relates to the system of purdah observed by many Muslim women, even in Bengal. In Amina's astonishingly secular answer, however, the term purdah refers to the restrictions imposed on all women, irrespective of community.

Osman agrees with her.

WHEN OSMAN ARRIVES at the hospital he is confronted with a prodigious puzzle.

'Package? What package? Was he carrying a package?'

'But of course, he was. It was a packed case that had come with him.'

'Wait. Let me check.'

Then half-an-hour later, 'No, there is no package. What was it? What did it contain?'

Even this does not strike Osman as strange as he thinks that they cannot have left it lying around and must have kept it stored in some safe place.

'How should I know what it contained? It was a case packed in gunny-cloth. Yesterday a phone call was made from here to the address where it was being taken. No one could say anything last night. So it had been decided that it would be opened today to see if there was any proof of identity inside. It may have been kept safely elsewhere.'

'Oh no, he had nothing with him. This list was made this morning. Here is his name, Ganesh, aged about twenty-one or twenty-two. . . .'

Osman asks eagerly, 'Then his identity has been confirmed?'

'Only his name, written in a tattoo on his arm. The list does not mention that he had luggage with him.'

'But what can have happened to it then?'

'I am telling you it was not there; and you are saying what can have happened to it! What do you mean by it? What is your name? Osman? Ganesh was his name. Then why are you having such a headache over him?'[24]

[24] The man at the hospital counter wants to ward off the uncomfortable questions being raised by Osman. He indirectly imputes an ulterior motive to them when he suggests that it is not normal for Osman, a Muslim, to take

Osman keeps quiet; then he says slowly, 'Who knows? The way things are happening, the head starts aching of itself'.

He feels a little pleased to see the gentleman drawing his brows together as if the insult has hit him to the quick.

HEMANTA IS PUTTING on his shirt in the morning before going out. Anurupa comes and stands with a long face in front of him.

'Where are you going out so early?'

'I have to go to Seeta'.

The cloud darkens on Anurupa's face.

'What about your tea?'

'I shall have it with Seeta'.

Anurupa breaks out in a deeply injured voice, 'What is all this you have started, Hema? Khoka has gone out without even telling me. Now you are also going out. Am I not to be told anything? Have I become so insignificant?'

'But I am still here, Ma. I would of course have told you'. Hemanta justifies himself while re-adjusting the buttons on his shirt. Is it some new reaction that Ma is showing this morning? He cannot believe that she would so soon lose control over herself and re-open her charter of complaints. It is not like her to give vent to her raw sentiments so directly either.

He says in a casual voice again, 'I have already told you that I am going out in the morning. I have to be early because I may not find Seeta at home otherwise; so I thought I would have tea with her. If your kettle is already boiling then I may as well have it right now'.

But Anurupa seems oblivious of Hemanta's words and carries

---

so much interest in Ganesh, a Hindu. Osman can do very little under the circumstances, but his sharp reply makes it plain that he rightly suspects that there is something fishy in this strenuous denial of the very existence of the package.

on, 'How many sides do I have to keep an eye on? For how long? Is it not enough that I have to earn money to run the household? Now over and above that I am expected to keep track of whatever whim you people come up with. I just cannot take it, I am telling you, Hema. You are the eldest; can you not keep an eye on your younger brother? The boy has slipped out without telling me. He hasn't even had anything to eat. Why can't you find him out and tell him off?'

'He must have just gone somewhere and will be back again. Why should I tell him off for that?'

'Try to understand, Hema. Slipping out once in a while all alone is another matter. He is a child after all. But yesterday he was asking me if he can go out and watch the fight on the road. I did not allow him. That is why he has run off this morning on the sly.'

'That is because you hold him back too much. The boys in the neighbourhood are all out there, how can Khoka stay back?'

'He might have told me.'

'He didn't because you would never have let him go. If he had gone in spite of you then you would have been even angrier with him for disobeying you. Don't you see he had not wanted to hurt you? I was also afraid last night that you would forbid me; then how could I have caused you pain?'

'Oh, now I understand. You are bent on disobeying me; you are just obliging me by asking permission!'

'Should one be disobliging to one's mother?'

Hemanta smiles. Anurupa too seems to have come back to her senses.

'Alright, do whatever you want. I shall soon retire from my domestic duties. Then everything will be up to the two of you!'

'Which two of us, Ma? Oh, you are thinking of your son's future wife? You have already taken stock of everything, Ma?'

How long can you go on avoiding the inevitable like this? Hemanta thinks as he walks along. This is but the opening bout, what is the ultimate outcome of such matches of familial affection?

Maybe things will ease out eventually on both sides; but Hemanta cannot be sure. Circumstances make men and women. That is why it is easier to go along with them and to shy away even from clashes that are inevitable. Those days are over for him. But how is he going to face the coming days? Perhaps he knows what he should do on the short term in this special situation. But then all that will have to be built anew from day to day in the lives of his mother, Rama, Khoka and himself, adjusting with the changing lives of other people, known and unknown, while holding on to the movement ahead, struggling to correct himself continually, failing because of his own timidity, saving other lives and his own out of the conflicting experiences of laughter and tears, joys and pains—he just cannot imagine where his path lies through them! This is not the time either to think about all that. . . ..

'But why not?' Seeta asks in surprise, 'If you have to think of all this, why should you not start from today? It does not mean that all other things are going to be driven out of your mind because of that! In that case it would be sheer poetry, not concrete thought. Can anyone be transformed in a single day? Even for a person who suddenly renounces home and opts out, it is the opting out that comes all at once, not the thought of renunciation. And as for you, you are not abandoning your family. Why don't you take your time to think? Let each day take care of itself, let today's work be done today, things will be sorted out'.

'What you are saying is that I should proceed cautiously . . .'.

'Yes, indeed. You in particular. Can you proceed anywhere with your mind running in every direction? Do not be angry, you always think of yourself as a loner. But there are others in the world as well; your thoughts and your practice have to be adjusted with theirs. How then can you change yourself all of a sudden?'

'How will Ma take it?'

'All that will be sorted out. It is not as if you are going to be or do something out of the ordinary altogether. You may think so, but the drama of life does not fit into your sense of the dramatic. Does this sound like advice?' Sita asks after a pause.

Hemanta says, 'May be, but even then it sounds good'.

'But really these words are not my advice to you, Hemanta. What is happening to you has also been happening to me for some time. I am really talking of what I myself have experienced. The terrible truth that I am slowly coming to terms with is that two years back I did not even know what my country is. Still, I was so full of arrogance about my patriotism'.

As they sit having tea together Hemanta discovers in Seeta's face the glow of fulfilment for having overcome her mistaken ideas; her eyes shine with the humility of simple conviction. Today itself, on his way here Hemanta has been agitated by the pricks of envy and frustration that riddle his relationship with Seeta and the corrosive thought that Seeta's true self has remained elusive for him, even that she herself has deliberately maintained her distance from him with her unfeeling designs. But right now, he feels many of these wounds healing up even while he has to admit Seeta's superiority to him. In fact, he realises in relief and gratitude that it was his own narrowness that had created the distance between them. Seeta had neither tried to draw him artfully towards her, nor had she created any deceptive distance with him. It was he who had tried to measure Seeta with his stunted and poor yardstick and been in confusion and misery. He has not even paid Seeta due respect for her directness and simplicity and instead of appreciating what she has, his tendency has been to trim her down to his small needs since after all, he has thought of her only as a woman.

'What are you mooning over? Drink up your tea', Seeta says in a somewhat embarrassed manner; it is embarrassing when you are laying bare the simplicity of your own actions and that seems to be in vain. She finishes her own tea and without making any attempt at elaborate introductions, asks straightaway: 'What was auntie's response?'

'Last night she took it quite well. But she was somewhat different this morning. I think Ma is a bit puzzled, or perhaps she is feeling very jealous'.

Seeta looks up at Hemanta and says, 'I know. When she came to me last night in search of you, she told me in so many words that I have turned you into a puppet; you are being guided by me. She has really come to believe it'.

Hemanta says helplessly, 'What can we do about it? Last night I had felt so relieved talking to her. This morning she spoilt my mood in five minutes. You are right; no one can change overnight'.

'No, Hemanta,' urges Seeta, 'we cannot brush it aside just by saying what can we do about it? You have to give her some time'.

'What do you mean?'

'Only that auntie must be given some time to understand and adjust. Yesterday I had felt annoyed at her blind love for her children which only hampers them. But I was wrong. I realize now that she may be blind; she may be under false impressions; but you cannot ignore it, nor can I. In a special situation, one hardly has breathing-time to think of family affections. When the issue is big, we cannot always count personal gains and losses. But this matter is somewhat different. Here it is just your intimacy with me that is causing the trouble. We cannot blame your mother or treat her with severity because she is not happy about it. She is not a selfish person and is only concerned about your welfare. She cannot quite place me in her scheme of things. But with time, perhaps she will be able to overcome this weakness. So I have something to say to you'.

'Say it then'.

'You must keep your distance from me for a time'.

'For how long?'

'Well, until auntie gets rid of this notion that you are under my thumb. It is not necessary to try to make her believe that you have expunged me from your mind altogether, nor to make a show of having made a big sacrifice; that is all'.

'But wouldn't that mean deluding her?'

'Not at all. Right now, even if we behave naturally towards each other she will twist it according to her distorted vision and will try to find fault with you for ignoring her at my beck and call. It will only feed her obsession. If she has time to think about it calmly, she will surely get over it. Think of her as a sick person and take care of her. That is surely not deluding her!'

Hemanta sits without a word. The lines of his face betray disappointment and distress. Seeta thinks sadly, perhaps Hemanta is working up within himself emotions of anguish at the thought of keeping distance from her. But she is relieved when he speaks. No, Hemanta is not so weak.

'I had need of you more than ever just now'.

'Oh no, that is where you are mistaken. If you need me all the time to prop you up in your resolution, it is better for it to collapse. But that is not going to happen. Your new confidence is not going to fail you and you will find many others who will be more helpful than I can be'. Seeta adds with a gentle smile: 'Any way did I say we are giving up seeing each other altogether?'

JAYANTA'S ONLY WORRY is that he will get a scolding from Ma when he gets home. All other fear has left him today. Together with ten or twelve other companions of his own age he is in a mood to conquer the world. He has played so many pranks in league with these neighbourhood boys, has had so many adventures from stealing flowers from the iron-grilled garden in front of Roybabu's house to letting loose Mr. Dickson's dog on the road; but never in his young life of twelve years has he experienced so much heady excitement. His intention in banding up with Sisir, Mana, Ashok and others had been to get home quickly after a brief survey of the surroundings; but it is almost midday now, and still they are on the road. All of them ran to the big crossing to see people setting fire to a military truck. Four other trucks have been burnt down so far and only now have they returned to the entrance of their own neighbourhood. How could they go back home while all this is happening? What is a bit of scolding after this? Thousands are on the road today, determined not to let a single vehicle pass; how can he go back home?

Sisir asks, 'Why are they not letting the cars pass, brother?'

Twelve-year-old Jayanta in his wisdom is surprised at this question of his nine-year-old friend and tells him, 'Don't you know? Why did they shoot? This is our country. We can do what we like. What right do they have to shoot?'

Ashok adds, 'We also want our freedom. Why should we be under them?'

Mana agrees, 'Dad says we are always fighting among ourselves. That is why we are not able to be free. So now we have got united. Can't you see?'

A vehicle of the Peace Squad with flags of the three political parties out to calm down the unruly crowds has stopped at the corner of the road; announcement is coming from loudspeakers: 'You cannot get justice or Independence by burning down cars. Maintain peace. Either go home or join the protest rally. Let us be united for our rights'.

Jayanta says, 'Did I not tell you, Mana, not to throw stones? Do you hear that?'

Now they are standing near the entrance to their lane. Their voices are hoarse with shouting 'Bande Mataram', 'Jai Hind', 'Inquilab zindabad!' Not to be ignored they have raised their voices in competition with adults. They are faint with hunger. But somehow, they have lost the will to get back to their respective homes inside the lane. Something like the fairy tales of their dreams is actually taking place on the main road over there; there is ample opportunity to behave like the heroes of those tales they have heard of.

Just near the corner, a military truck is on fire. They stop to have a look. A vehicle carrying army personnel is coming in this direction. They can hear it approaching.

Jayanta orders in a firm voice like an army commander, 'This is the last time. We go home once they hear us. Do what I tell you. Move forward. Ready? Inquilab Zindabad! Jai Hind! Bande Mataram! Inquilab. . . .'

Jayanta leans back towards Mana and crashes heavily on the road. He moves a few times trying to get up, then coughs blood and finally goes limp. Thirteen children carry him inside the lane and lay him down on the first verandah they can find.

Just at that moment, Anurupa, in growing impatience, walks down the lane in search of her son.

IT IS ALMOST half-past eight, but Ajoy seems to be in no hurry to take his bath. He is still absorbed in talking with Sudhir and Niranjan, talk that has started since he came back from his daily trip to the market. It seems he has forgotten that he has to reach office by ten and it takes more than an hour to get there. If he is thinking of using public transport today instead of walking up to Howrah Bridge, he has every right to do that; to make a splurge occasionally by spending money that way is nothing one may object to. But he should have the sense that he might be late for office even after wasting all that money if he does not get ready now.

His whole family starts feeling slightly uncomfortable, except for Madhu. All of them except Madhu wonder what there is to talk about at such length with these erstwhile classmates now that he has got a job while they are still students. He should not be so chummy with them anymore.

Ananta, unable to stand the tension, tells his daughter, 'Madhu, go and call him once more'.

'But I called him just now'.

'Call him again. What's the time? Half-past eight? Tell him it is quarter to nine'.

'I have already told him once. Do you think he has no sense of time? What is the use of pestering him?' Madhu says calmly.

These days she has cast aside the restlessness that had possessed her during the years when negotiations for her marriage had been falling through one after another. It seems she has rooted out all hopes of that nature and has found peace at last.

Ananta beats his own forehead with his palm and says, 'Just stop giving me advice, Madhu, why don't you go and hang yourself!'

'Why don't you find me some rope, father? Even that needs money. It took me one hour to clean and shampoo the hair of the daughter-in-law of the Duttas, and she gave me just four annas for it. Too little for buying a rope. Let me start earning a bit more; then I shall get myself one!' Madhu only laughs as she says this.

Ananta looks at his daughter suspiciously out of the corner of his eyes.

He feels astounded looking at his own children. Deprivation stalks his family; there is frustration all around, and yet they seem bent on not minding him at all. With the War over he has been unceremoniously thrown out of the office where he had been working; the kitchen fires are burning only because his son has given up his studies and has managed to get a job; the sari Madhu is wearing is so worn that one is ashamed to look at it; Ajoy's office dress is no different from what workmen wear; his blood goes cold when he thinks of the future and yet the children seem to be unmindful of all that. Time was when the household could be managed more smoothly and there was still hope that somehow, they would be able to tide over the problems of Ajoy's education and Madhu's marriage. Then these people were depressed and in despair all the time; outbursts of mutual recrimination, blows, tears and quarrels were everyday affairs. Now the situation is far worse and yet –look at them—they seem to have given up all hopes for future and unmindful of their half-filled stomachs and frayed clothes, have grown much livelier in their desperation. Nothing to fear, we shall be able to face all this and live it down, is their present attitude. There was a time when Madhu, unable to endure the daily abuses of her mother, had tried to slash her own throat with a razor. If Ajoy had not stopped her in time the worst could have happened. She still carries that mark on her throat. But now she does not mind however much you may abuse her and mock at her. Far from bursting in anger, she just laughs it all away.

And yet, the fact is that the sari she is wearing does not bear looking at.

He nods sleepily for a while, fancifully thinking that it is better to seek pardon of the children and admit that this is how it should be.

Then he suddenly sits up and thunders, Ajoy, don't you have office today? What is all this idle gossip going on?

Ajoy comes in and replies, 'I am not going to the office today, Dad. All offices and factories are on strike. All public transport is off the road'.

Ananta sits up in excited anxiety and fear. He shouts, 'Go at once. Don't you wait for food now! Get something on your way if you feel hungry. Go on foot, never mind if you reach late. Dropping out on any other day is no big matter, but today you have to be there. Tell Manager Sahib that you reached with great difficulty because tramcars and buses are not plying. You must say some people had tried to prevent you forcibly from attending office, but you still made your way after much trouble without listening to them . . .'.

Ananta starts coughing; breathing with great difficulty he goes on, 'Go! Go! Sahib will be pleased with you; he will raise your salary; you shall be promoted!'

Bout of coughing over, he lies still with his limbs drawn in like one dead of exertion.

Madhu fans him; Ajoy rubs his chest and back. Niranjan who has come in to see what the matter is stands with eyes downcast. Even when Madhu skilfully keeps herself covered in her torn sari, one has to keep one's eyes averted from her. Now in her distress she has become unmindful of her modesty.

Half-an-hour later, Ananta feeling a little better, calls Ajoy.

'Yes, Dad?'

'Do not go to office today. If no one is going, it would not be proper for you to go. It is better to be with the others'.

'Niru-da, don't leave. I have something to tell you', says Madhu as she goes to the inner room to change into her only undamaged sari.

Niranjan tells Ananta, 'You should take some medicine for your cough'.

'There are so many things we should do, my boy, but do they get done?' Ananta says with chagrin.

'I have wanted to call Doctor Pal so many times, but you always refuse', Ajay says gently not in a tone of complaint against him, but to comfort him.

Ananta corrects himself and replies, 'It is not necessary to call him. I can go myself. Point is that the medicines do not suit me'.

Madhu has put on her only whole sari. Now she comes out and tells Niranjan, 'You had said you would introduce me to Mr. Ghosh's family; will you take me today? I can start working tomorrow, or even from evening today'. She smiles a little diffidently, 'the only thing I am worried about is would they like my cooking? After all, they are so rich!'[25]

Ananta stares at her. He has not given his consent; actually he has forbidden her; yet without referring to him at all his daughter is standing right in front of him and requesting her brother's friend to get her hired as a cook at somebody's house! Does she have no

[25] Madhu is trying to get a job as a cook in an affluent household against her father's wishes. Apparently she did not get an opportunity like her brother to attend college and therefore lacks qualification for an office job. Even the fact that plans to marry her off have not been fruitful is turned into her own failure at home so that she is regarded by her parents as a useless burden on the family even when she takes a large share in the housework. When she realises this, she shakes off the middle-class prejudices of her family and decides to make a livelihood of her own even if it may be regarded as being beneath the dignity of the family. Ajoy however is sympathetic to her and feels guilty because she could not have the same opportunity that he had.

shame, no sense of humiliation? Ajay fixes his eyes on the floor. The red cemented floor is kept spick and span by Madhu who scrubs it clean twice a day. Though not ashamed of Madhu earning money as cook or domestic servant he finds his ears tingling with vexation because she has to do so in spite of his being there.

'But it cannot be done today, Madhu!'

'Why? Are cooks also having a day off today?'

Niranjan smiles at this and says, 'We have to go right now. Where is the time for breathing today? We are having a small meeting here and then there is the big rally; who knows where we may be needed after that?'

'Does that mean dada is going with you too? Then take me with you. I also want to look around and see what is happening'.

With shining eyes Madhu says 'I am not in a mood to stay home. I feel I have to go somewhere or do something'.

EVEN ON THE train, they get to hear in confused bits and pieces of the troubles that have erupted in Calcutta. There has been firing since yesterday, fights have broken out in places, terrible things are going on. Today's morning papers carry yesterday's news. Even in their compartment five or six people had bought Bengali papers and read them out for everybody's benefit. Stories of developments today are spreading by word of mouth. As the train nears Calcutta, with each stop the stories branch out and thicken.

Troubles in Calcutta? Troubles in that big city? It bothers Ganesh's mother and she worries lest something should happen to Ganesh.

Jadav puts her fears to rest, 'Why should anything happen to Ganesh? There are millions and millions of people there; out of all of them why should trouble come to your Ganesh alone?'

She has asked at least ten or twelve times so far, 'Have you got Ganesh's letter with you? The letter where his address is written?'

He has already had it read out to him at least by ten people to whom he has shown it and knows it by heart by now so that it would not matter even if he lost it; but still Jadav carefully pulls out the neatly folded postcard from the pocket of his torn kurta once more and looks at it just to reassure himself and says: 'Look, here it is; didn't I tell you?'

The big railway station and the road outside the station into which they walk leave Jadav completely dazed. He has come to the city two or three times, but on those earlier occasions he had felt bewildered and frightened out of his wits by the humming crowds of people and the unending movement of vehicles on the road; today it seems to him by comparison as if the city has been put to sleep by some spell. People are scattered here and there, they seem to be in no hurry, however, but are rather waiting with bated breath. Outside, the flow of traffic is just nowhere to be seen. Jadav would not have felt so astounded if he had woken up one morning to find that the river next to their village had vanished.

'I think, Ganesh's mother, we shall have to go on foot'.

'What else? We have to go anyway, haven't we?'

Rani says, 'Why don't you ask someone which way to go?'

'Let us cross the bridge first, then I shall find someone'.

'Then hurry up and let us follow the others taking the same way! We don't want to be left here all by ourselves, do we?'

They have very little luggage with them; what luggage should people of their sort have, people who consider it good fortune if they get enough rice a day to cook in an earthen pot? Jadav carries the small bedding under his left arm because the ache in his right arm has increased with the jerking of the train and it feels numb right now. Ganesh's mother carries little Mana in the crook of her hip and lifts in her arm the bundle which contains four seers of rice and a couple of aubergines from her field. Rani takes hold of two-year-old Kali and carries the bamboo casket which contains their clothes and a few utensils. That child has slept enough and eaten her fill and even then goes on whining inconsolably as if she still yearns for something to eat and some place to sleep.

'Where are you going?'

Rani makes a face. It is that spectacled gentleman wearing a coat and sporting burnished shoes, that same lewd gentleman who had been leering and leering at her as if he would lick her naked body under her sari with his very eyes.

He seems to be a bit taken aback when Jadav tells him of the address they are looking for: 'It is quite a distance; how can you go so far? On another day it would have been different. But all the roads are blocked today. Police are firing. Bricks are being thrown at them; cars are burning; you will be killed if you try'.

'It is my son's address. We are going to see him'.

'But it is impossible today', says the gentleman emphatically 'See what trouble you have stepped into, coming straight from the countryside!'

Then he continues gravely, as if coming to the proposal with reluctance after much consideration: 'You cannot go there today. There is a way though, my residence is quite close. You can stay there tonight and look for your son a couple of days later when these troubles are over. I can even try to send your son the information . . .'.

Rani bursts out: 'Why keep standing, dad? We have a long way to go and we must reach dada's address today. Come on, let us get going . . .'.

Jadav takes a look at the man's face; really it is not a face to be trusted. Indeed, his eyes are fixed on Rani.

'Whether we live or die we have to reach my son's place today, babu'.

'What are you waiting for?' Rani admonishes him as she starts to move away. Jadav starts walking too, and turning his head for a moment finds the babu gazing at the beauty of the Ganges from the corner of the bridge puffing at his cigarette with an air of unconcern.

Once they have crossed the bridge, Jadav cannot feel sure if the babu was trying to make fools of them by concocting stories or whether he had only wanted to take advantage of the real situation. At this end of the road, a big truck burns like tinder. On that side, the charred remains of two smaller vehicles are lying. The road is strewn with stones and brickbats. Along one side of the road, some white military officers and a Gorkha contingent seem to be taking stock of the situation while the road opposite is choked with crowds, whose uproar resembles the thunder of twenty tigers roaring together.

Is it possible for them to move ahead through this?

Among the people milling around him, stands a young man in a shirt made from cut-piece and a cheap shawl, a young man who seems to come from a poor but genteel family. Taking a sharp look at him, Jadav takes the postcard from his pocket. Before he can come sufficiently close, however, the young man starts walking, not towards the turning to the left where the big crowds brim over into the main road, but to the right where the military officers have taken possession of the almost empty streets.

Ajoy had come to Howrah Station to meet the relative of an injured boy in the hospital to inform him about the latter's condition which was critical. The relative has not come, or maybe they have missed each other. On his way back after crossing the bridge he stops as a weird and intolerable scene meets his eye. The crowds have gathered on this side of the road, the other side is virtually empty; who would care to cross the road at the risk of his life? The road is strewn with stones and brickbats and a number of men obviously of the middle class have been forcibly mobilised to clean it up.[26] A young man in a blue and white striped shirt is

[26] This episode has been said to have a reference to the author's personal experience of the sheer repression unleashed by the army and the police in the aftermath of the popular upsurge of Rashid Ali Day. Not only were there indiscriminate arrests and lathi charges in the neighbourhoods of the troubled areas, but on the next morning ordinary people walking along the roads were forcibly recruited to clean up the roads. Manik Bandyopadhyay was sought to be similarly pressed into work. When he refused and

dragged down from the pavement by one squat officer with ginger whiskers and pressed to work. Do they not realise that it is wrong to take it lying down? Is an order enough to make them get down to cleaning the road without uttering a word? Ajoy now feels it is his fault that they are swallowing this insult without complaint. He too has to go up the same road; it is because he does not want to get into trouble that he has been standing here agape all this time. It is not as if nobody is going along that road and it is only some of them who are being pressed into work. His only worry is that they may catch hold of him too and then there will be a showdown because he is not going to obey their order on any account.

How can he go on dithering like a coward? He is not here to make trouble; he needs to go on that road which is not out of bounds in any way. He has a right to go. If he is himself afraid of abstaining from the unethical and of standing up for his rights, then what is so strange about those people starting to clean up the road without demur?

Ajoy moves ahead.

'Hoi!' The same officer with ginger whiskers marches straight up to him and orders him to clean up.

'Is this road closed to traffic?'

Ginger Whiskers is annoyed to be questioned, but keeping his temper in check, says peremptorily in Hindi: 'Go on! Clean up! Clean up! You have made this mess; you must clean it up!'

Ajoy says in English: 'You are mad!'

The man gives Ajay such a push with both hands that he is flung on the road. He hits his head slightly as he falls prone and finds a piece of brick near his right hand. Not brick made of burnt clay, but a hard piece of flagstone of the kind with which roads are paved. Momentarily Ajay sees red. He can move his right arm well enough. If he throws the brick now it can easily smash Ginger

---

confronted the police sergeant, he was pushed and thrown down on the road for his intransigence, like the fictional Ajoy.

Whisker's skull. Let anything happen after that.

'No', Ajoy whispers through clenched teeth, 'No!' He is well brought-up. He cannot act under blind impulse because of a personal insult. He remembers the faces of the injured boys at the hospital. He recalls the youthful faces of those sitting in blockade on the road. Even Satan from hell cannot break down his resolve. He must remain calm.

Slowly he stands up. His left arm may have been fractured. But this is not the time to worry about that; no doubt it will mend.

Ginger Whiskers stares at him. He has seen the brick Ajoy had raised to throw at his head and which he is now putting down. Why did he not throw it? He might have died if he had been hit by it. But what stopped the fellow? Ginger Whiskers stares on perhaps because it is too much for him to comprehend.

Standing up, Ajoy finds himself almost surrounded by a family evidently from the countryside. They are asking him: 'Did you get hurt? Are you badly hurt, Babu?'

'No. I am fine'.

Then Jadav shows him the postcard asking him: 'How can we get here, Babu?'

'Please wait a little', Ajoy says without looking either at him or the postcard.

After a while he starts to walk, then pauses and asks Jadav: 'Yes, what is it?'

He reads the postcard and says, 'Do you know Dalhousie Square? Laldighi?'

'Laldighi? Laldighi? I think so, Babu.'

'Good. Then it is easy. You go to the east side of Laldighi. There are two roads, one from the north-east side and the other from the south-east side. You can take either of the two roads towards the east. Is that clear?'

Jadav shakes his head in incomprehension.

'Why not? You will find just two roads to the east, not ten. If you go via Lalbazar you will reach Bowbazar crossing and then have to turn left and if you go via Mission Row you will be crossing the tram-track; then you just have to ask someone again . . .'

Silently Jadav takes the postcard back.

Ajay says severely, 'Then you have to come with me. I am going towards Laldighi myself. But I am following this route. This is the only route. If you come with me you may get into trouble and you have women with you. So consider that.'

Rani says, 'Let us go then.'

Ajoy walks in long strides and crosses Ginger Whiskers. This time the latter merely looks on and lets Ajoy be. After he has gone some distance, he becomes aware of Jadav and his family following him and pauses for them. Then he walks on. But he has to stop once more. His vexed face makes Jadav feel uncomfortable. But by now he is able to believe without reservation that this young man is of a different category from those urbane charmers who go round setting up traps for credulous country yokels.

Once in an attempt at apology he says, 'You have to walk a long way for us!'

'Not really. I would have to walk anyway; this is just somewhat more. What is to be done? You have got hold of me, haven't you?'

Keeping the iron sheds of the river jetty to their right they walk straight on. All around there is silence without the movements of daily life, an atmosphere of breathless waiting everywhere. In between the sheds Rani can catch glimpses of foreign ships with their giant funnels. They become invisible before she can have an eyeful.

They have to walk a long way; however apart from being footsore they are able to find Electricals Limited without much trouble. But they are flabbergasted to find it shuttered and closed. 'All is lost!' says Jadav.

Ajoy says in annoyance, 'Something must be wrong with your address. What more can I do? You find your own way now, I am going!'

But even after saying this he stays on. His heart is eager to go and join the rally, but how can he leave these poor people on the lurch? He takes the postcard once more from Jadav and verifies the address. Nothing is wrong with the address. This is the shop where Ganesh works. Now the address of the owner has to be obtained. The owner would know Ganesh's whereabouts.

Ajoy has found burgeoning within him a liking for the unknown Ganesh whose letter written in big unsteady characters he has read. Every line of that letter, with its uncouth wording and grammatical mistakes, speaks of his love for his parents and his siblings and contains hints of the hard struggle he is carrying out in this big city to keep them alive. Breathing optimism in his letter to his family Ganesh has proved his courage and self-confidence in adversity. But his intelligence cannot be commended. He has only given the address of his workplace; he should have mentioned where he has been residing.

But Ajoy is reassured once he is able to find the gatekeeper and get the necessary information from him. Ganesh is not lacking in intelligence. The owner of Electricals Limited lives on the floor above the shop and Ganesh has been living in. Jadav and his family are also relieved when they learn this.

Rani says happily, 'Oh dear! So we are safe! We were in such panic!'

Ajoy says, 'So can I leave now?'

Jadav responds in deep gratitude, 'Certainly, Babu, go your way. You have really done a lot for us'.

Bending his head in acknowledgement of their gratefulness, Ajoy proceeds on his way without further ado.

Jadav requests the gatekeeper respectfully to call Ganesh.

The gatekeeper however could not have cared less. He says casually, 'Who knows if he is in or has gone out. Why don't you go up yourselves and see?'

When Dasgupta is told that Ganesh's parents have come looking for him he is none too pleased and comes up himself to meet them. He already knows the story he has to tell about Ganesh.

Ganesh has run away with some goods from the shop; he is a thief. The police have been informed and if he is caught, he would be put in jail. They must be frightened off with this story so that they do not make trouble. It is not as if he fears exposure any longer, but if Ganesh chose to die of a bullet like a fool why should Dasgupta be subjected to even the smallest amount of bother over that? He has enough trouble to deal with even as it is. It irritates him to think that he might have to spend even ten minutes in the business of investigation into Ganesh's death.

The family huddles close to one another near the entrance of the flat. Rani stands carrying her little brother on her hip, prominent in her slightly arched pose. As soon as she catches his eye, the eye measures her from head to foot and even registers the faintly offended look on her face. Dasgupta's mind begins to flow in a different direction all at once. Standing upon his prestige he yawns heavily and changes his expression into one of grave unconcern.

'Looking for Ganesh, are you?'

Jadav says, 'Yes, sir! He is here, isn't he?'

Dasgupta avoids the question and asks instead: 'Are you related to him?'

No, it would not do to frighten them with the story of Ganesh's supposed theft. He tries to think of some other story which would serve his purpose better.

'Ganesh is my son, Babu. We are coming from the countryside.'

'Is that so?' Dasgupta says in a detached manner, 'But Ganesh is not here.'

'When will he return, Babu?'

'Actually, he has taken leave for a few days. He has gone to some place; he had told me, but I cannot recall just now. He has made some friends and he has gone with a bunch of them. He will be surely back in three or four days.'

By this time Ganesh's body may have already started to rot at the hospital or in the morgue; but Dasgupta feels not the slightest compunction to inform his parents and his siblings that he would surely return in three or four days. His glibness however Rani finds just a little discordant.

Jadav says disheartened, 'Then we are in trouble; where can we go?'

'Why did you have to descend here foolishly all of a sudden without fixing up something?'

Dasgupta says curtly with a show of displeasure. Then he pretends to consider it for a while and says assuming reluctance: 'Stay here for the time being. What else is there to do?'

But even as he says it, he cannot check himself from glancing at Rani.

'Our doctor's son is there, dad. If we go to him, he will make some arrangement for us', Rani intervenes.

Jadav is hesitant. Keshab Doctor's son lives in Howrah. It would not be easy walking back all the way. Then they may not even find him at home, what would be their plight then?

Dasgupta continues, 'Stay here, where can you go now? I can arrange one room for all of you.'

Rani says, 'Dad, come this side'. When Jadav is close to her, she whispers in a low voice, 'No, dad, we cannot stay here. This babu is not a good person. I do not think he can be trusted. If there is some trouble dada might lose his job'.

Jadav turns to Dasgupta and says, 'Sir, a gentleman from our village has given us a letter of reference to his son. It is better to go to him than to give you trouble'.

'As you please', says Dasgupta thinking to himself that times are bad indeed.

They slowly descend on the road again. They have to go back a long way even beyond Howrah Station. They move towards Laldighi along the same way by which they had come.

Ganesh's mother wonders, 'Ganesh has taken leave and has gone somewhere! Where has he gone then? He never mentioned it in his letter, did he? I just cannot understand what is happening!'

Jadav says angrily, 'Your son now has cronies in the city!'

'You must never say that about Ganesh! My son is not of that sort!'

As they come towards the crossing from where they have to turn towards Laldighi, the far-off tumult of people reaches their ears.

They have to stop as they approach Laldighi. The pressure of gathering crowds is such that it is impossible to make their way through it. The head of a mammoth rally is turning the corner of Laldighi. Three huge flags of three different colours are dancing in the northerly wind. The tail-end of the rally is not in sight. Slogans are on the air from a thousand voices. It seems to Jadav as if tigers are roaring in jubilation.

Suddenly they find Ajoy, standing in front of them.

They push through the crowds to reach him. Jadav calls out, Babu!

But Ajoy cannot hear him. Jadav finds him talking to himself: 'Yes, we have moved on! They have not been able to stop us! We are moving on indeed!'

Ajoy's head is held high and his eyes are shining with exuberance of joy. As Jadav looks on, he finds him breaking into a smile. The sun seems to be rising on his face as the clouds are being rolled back.

MANIK BANDYOPADHYAY (birth name Prabodh Kumar Bandyopadhyay, 19 May 1908–3 December 1956) is a major figure of twentieth-century Bengali literature. He authored 38 novels and 306 stories. His best-known works include *Padma Nadir Majhi* (The Boatman on the River Padma, 1936), *Putul Nacher Itikatha* (The Puppet's Tale, 1936), *Shahartali* (Suburbia, 1941), *Chatushkone* (The Quadrilateral, 1948), *Swadhinatar Swad* (Taste of Freedom 1951) and *Halud Nadi Sabuj Ban* (Yellow River Green Forest 1956). He was born in Dumka, Santal Parganas. His father was a government official who was transferred all over Bengal, giving young Manik a wide exposure to diverse places, cultures, dialects, and people. He became a member of the Progressive Writers' Association in the early 1940s, and joined the Communist Party of India in 1944. In ill health and plagued by financial problems, he died at the early age of 48. His unfailing commitment to his creative objective gave him an iconic status as an 'engaged' author, a 'pen-wielding proletarian', according to the author's own description.

MALINI BHATTACHARYA (b. 1943) retired as Professor of English and Director, School of Women's Studies, Jadavpur University, Kolkata. She is a well-known activist in the women's movement, and is President of the All India Democratic Women's Association. She is a prolific author, translator, playwright, and poet. She was elected to the Lok Sabha as a Communist Party of India (Marxist) candidate from the Jadavpur constituency in 1989, and re-elected in 1991.